THE STRAY RELATION

ANNE CLEELAND

OTHER HISTORICAL
ADVENTURES BY ANNE
CLEELAND:

Tainted Angel
Daughter of the God-King
The Bengal Bridegift
The Barbary Mark
The True Pretender
A Death in Sheffield
The Spanish Mask
The Gypsy Queen
The Blighted Bride

For Finn's mom, who can out-think the rest of us; and for all others like her.

CHAPTER 1

Lisabetta was feeding the chickens in the Abbey's barnyard and idly wondering if they would have sufficient fish for the evening meal—she should arrange for another delivery, perhaps, when she spoke to Antoine the fishmonger. It was amusing, that she was dealing with such mundane matters whilst the world was teetering on the precipice, but she'd found that there was great satisfaction to be had, in performing everyday tasks.

At present, she was hiding out—as she'd done many times before—here at the Abbey Beaulieu, a place well-suited for hiding out since it was located in the hills that surrounded the French town of Strasbourg, just across the Rhine River from Prussia. The Abbey's location on this particular section of the Rhine also meant that it was well-suited for the gathering and dispersing of information—something the Abbot of Beaulieu had used to his advantage, during the recent war. And small blame to him for staying vigilant; it was essential to keep careful track of the ever-shifting allegiances that were in play, now that Napoleon had been captured, and a war-weary Europe was trying to sort itself out.

Hard on this thought, the figure of Dom Julian himself appeared at the courtyard gate—wearing ordinary black wool garments, since he was now prohibited from wearing his habit and cowl.

His attitude, as he waited for her to acknowledge him, was one of subtle contrition, and—to show that she bore no ill feelings—she rested the wooden bowl on a hip, and teased, "So; am I in need of a further scolding? Shall I tell the chickens to cover their ears?"

With a small smile, he acknowledged, "I wanted to apologize; I was unduly harsh."

"No matter," she replied, as she began spreading the chicken feed again. "It was only an idea, and not a very good one—I panicked a bit, I think. I will come up with another plan."

"Yes; and I do not wish to add to your distress, but you have a visitor."

Lisabetta lifted her brows in surprise; she'd been an operative during the war—it helped that she was a beautiful woman, and well-placed to gather-up the secrets of powerful men—but at present she was in hiding, and any unexpected visitor would be unwelcome. Since the Abbot would well-know this, she stated the obvious. "And you believe it is someone I should see."

In an even tone, he replied, "It is the Englishman, and so I dare not send him away."

This was of interest—and not wholly unexpected—and so she turned the wooden bowl over, unceremoniously dumping the remainder of the chicken feed on the hard-packed earth. "I will see him. Let me wash, first."

She moved to pass through the gate that led to the Abbey's garden, and he fell into step beside her. "Shall I insist that I be present? I can tell him I won't allow you to be unchaperoned."

She smiled at this absurdity, since the Englishman knew better than most that she was no virtuous maiden. "No need; I do not fear him."

They continued through the garden and toward the small outbuilding that served as the women's quarters—or which used to, back when the place was a functioning Abbey. In a grave tone, he urged, "Perhaps you should be reconsider, Lisabetta; everything has changed, with the news of Josephine's death."

This was undisputedly true, and especially for Lisabetta. Even though Napoleon had been captured and exiled, his former Empress continued to wield a great deal of power in Paris—especially amongst those who longed to see the Emperor return to his former glory. But she'd died—rather unexpectedly—just as she was entertaining a visit from the Tsar of Russia, which seemed a bit ominous, since the Tsar held no fondness for the exiled Emperor. And although the Abbey was isolated atop its hill, word of the Empress' death had reached them almost immediately; the Abbot made certain that he was kept abreast, and this was troubling news indeed.

"We shall see," Lisabetta replied, with a fine show of unconcern. "I doubt that he will attempt to seize me out-of-hand."

Apparently, her companion did not share her optimism. "If you wish to disappear down the river, I can stall him for an hour."

In some amusement, she glanced up at him. "The Englishman has eyes and ears everywhere, *mon Abbé*; it is far safer that I remain behind these walls."

"As you wish."

Because his tone implied that he did not necessarily agree, she added in a practical manner, "Besides, if I flee, it will only serve to raise his alarm; far better to face him down, and hear what he has to say."

Dom Julian warned, "He is a dangerous man, Lisabetta."

"Ah, but I am a dangerous woman," she countered with a smile. "He well-knows this, and we respect each other. You must have no fears."

Her companion bowed his head in reluctant acquiescence. "Very well. I will put him in the visitor's parlor."

"Yes—I will hurry along; he is one who does not like waiting."

She parted from him at the door to the woman's quarters; the Abbey Beaulieu was not technically an Abbey, anymore—when Napoleon had ruled France as Emperor, he'd seized all the monasteries so as to lessen the Catholic Church's power. This particular Abbey, however, had been allowed to continue as a beggar's hostel—so long as it was made clear that it was no longer a place of worship, and—more importantly—made no further contributions to the Church's coffers.

Napoleon would have been very much surprised, however, to discover that the Abbot of Beaulieu continued on much as he'd done before—under his new guise as the hostel's Director—and with many of the former monks now being housed here as beggars. No one had seen fit to challenge this sleight-of-hand, mainly because those that knew would keep the secret, and Dom Julian was careful never to attract any unwanted attention their way.

The need for secrecy had lessened, of course, now that Napoleon was in exile, but the Abbey continued in its guise as a hostel for the poor; it paid to be cautious, after the turmoil of the past twenty years. After all, there were persistent rumors that Napoleon was plotting his escape from the Island of Elba, and therefore it remained paramount that no rumor of these particular beggars—or of their activities—ever be allowed to reach his ears.

The Abbey had assigned Lisabetta a proctor during her stay—a thin, supercilious man who was tasked with looking after her—and although this gentleman was always annoyingly underfoot, she always treated him with great courtesy; he was often an excellent source for the threads of information that she gathered.

At present, the proctor was slicing vegetables in the kitchen and she approached to inform him, "I am told I have a visitor in the visitor's parlor; if you would be good enough to provide me escort, monsieur." Vestiges of the Abbey's protocols still remained, and an unmarried female had to be escorted when she ventured onto the premises of the Abbey proper.

The proctor paused in his task to lift his brows in surprise. "Oh? Who would come here, mademoiselle?"

"I will see; he looks to be an ordinary gentleman," she replied, and smiled to herself at this massive understatement. "Let me wash, first."

After splashing water from the washbasin onto her face, Lisabetta dried herself with the coarse, home-spun cloth and thoughtfully regarded her image in the small dressing-mirror. Despite her light words, what Dom Julian had said was true; everything had changed, with the Empress Josephine's death. It would pay to be wary; she was now very much at-risk.

It also meant that she could expect a variety of suitors to promptly show an interest—men who would be far more interested in her rumored dowry than her suitability as a wife—and who could blame them? Everyone could be forgiven for believing she'd lead her husband on a merry dance, given her reputation, but—as was often the case—where there were riches to be had, such concerns were easily discounted.

Still and all, it looked to be an interesting month —if she managed to survive it—and finally, *finally* she held the opportunity to arrange matters more to her liking, even though she knew she'd have to step carefully; he was a very shrewd player, and one who was well-familiar with her methods.

With this in mind, she kept her expression pleasant as she was escorted into the visitor's parlor, and—upon sighting her visitor—dipped a demure curtsey. "Monsieur."

Her visitor was a slender man who wore merchant's clothing—a rather nondescript fellow, save for a pair of keen grey eyes that assessed her shrewdly. And despite his ordinary appearance, Lisabetta knew—from long experience—that he wasn't ordinary; not in the least. This unassuming gentleman was England's spymaster, and he and Lisabetta had something of an ambiguous history together; whilst she'd generally acted as an operative for France during the war, on occasion she'd been willing to ally with his interests, so long as she would not be compromised. And so long as she was handsomely paid, of course.

"We are old friends; no need to stay," she informed her proctor, who bowed his head and exited, discreetly closing the door behind him.

Lisabetta and the grey-eyed man regarded each other for a moment, before he bowed his head politely. "My condolences on the death of your father's wife."

With a wry smile, she gestured for him to come

join her at the carved mahogany table that centered the room. "You may mock me as much as you wish, monsieur; I am immune."

He took off his gloves, and as he laid them on the table alongside his hat, he remarked, "You can't help but wonder what they would have to say to each other in the afterlife—your father, and his wedded wife. Although I very much doubt they've landed in the same place."

Lisabetta's father had been the Empress Josephine's first husband, the Vicomte de Beauharnais. His marriage to Josephine had not been a happy one, and he'd essentially lived a separate life, surrounded by a variety of mistresses. One of his favorites, Madame de Grère, had birthed Lisabetta and her older sister, Eugenie.

In the same wry tone, Lisabetta answered, "I imagine Josephine would thank my father on bended knees for being so conveniently guillotined, so that she was free when she caught the Emperor's eye."

He spread his hands in acknowledgment. "Few would argue that she wasn't fortunate in her husband's execution." There was a slight pause. "She was also fortunate to escape the same fate as he; one wonders what she offered in exchange for her life, when she was held prisoner at Carmes."

"One does wonder," Lisabetta agreed, matching his mild tone.

He regarded her with a thoughtful eye. "Your own mother was very fortunate in turn; she managed to escape from Mainz—and just before the Prussian coalition destroyed the St. Albans Abbey."

Lisabetta decided she may as well get to the point. "I do not know where the St. Alban's treasure is, monsieur," she advised him. "To my deep regret."

He watched her for a few moments, his impassive grey eyes concealing his thoughts. "There are many who believe you do know—de Gilles, amongst them."

She smiled, slightly. "I regret to inform you that Seigneur de Gilles is mistaken."

There was a small silence which was nonetheless heavy with meaning. Twenty years earlier, during France's bloody revolution, Lisabetta had been but a young girl when her mother had managed to escape the siege of Mainz with her two daughters, and flee up the Rhine River. Mainz had long been considered a strategic city for military purposes, with its origins going all the way back to the Romans; indeed, the venerable St. Albans Abbey had existed there for nearly a thousand years until it was—unfortunately—destroyed.

But Mainz had fallen to the Prussians during the siege, and almost immediately rumors arose that Lisabetta's duplicitous father—a general in the French Revolutionary Army, who'd been tasked with defending Mainz—had instead brokered a deal to allow the city to be surrendered to the Prussians in exchange for some or all of the fabled St. Albans treasure—Roman gold, along with jewels and priceless artifacts which were believed to have been hidden beneath the Abbey's ancient sanctuary floor.

No one knew if this rumor was true, only that ensuing events seem to verify it; the Vicomte de Beauharnais had weakly defended Mainz—surprising, for a man of his military acumen—and the foundations of St. Albans had been breached during the siege, at about the same time that the man's favorite mistress had managed to disappear with her two little girls.

As a result of these rumors, when de Beauharnais returned to Paris he was promptly thrown into prison by Robespierre, who also arrested the man's estranged wife, Josephine. And in an ironic twist of fate, De Beauharnais was executed a mere five days before the end of the Revolution—some said because he'd refused to tell Robespierre of the treasure's whereabouts.

In the meantime, Lisabetta's mother—Madame de Grère, who also hailed from Josephine's Island of Martinique—had apparently brokered her own deal so as to keep herself and her daughters alive. The exact parameters of the deal were unknown, but as a result of it, Josephine was released from Carmes Prison and Madame de Grère—along with her two daughters—were allowed to live very comfortable lives, despite their dubious alliance with the disgraced de Beauharnais.

Indeed, when Madame de Grère had died some years later, the two daughters found themselves under the direct protection of Josephine herself—

now the Empress of France. Josephine was known to be loyal to those who'd come to her aid, and the fact that the two sisters were her first husband's illegitimate children didn't test that loyalty in the slightest.

And so, those who'd followed this particular chain of events could be forgiven for believing that the rumors where true, and that de Beauharnais had indeed confiscated the treasure of St. Alban's, and then had secreted it with his favorite mistress rather than hand it over to the notorious Committee of Public Safety.

But now, the death of Josephine—rather unexpected, as the former Empress was not known to be sickening—was no doubt what had brought this rather alarming visitor to Lisabetta's door. After eight long years of war, the treasuries of all the countries who'd fought against Napoleon were thoroughly depleted, and if—as was rumored—hostilities were to resume, each would be desperately looking for new funding of any kind. With Lisabetta's powerful protectress dead, there would be a renewed interest in her connection to the fabled treasure.

Her visitor's next words seemed to confirm this, as he bluntly advised, "With Josephine's death, you will no longer be protected from those who may seek to force you to reveal what you know."

Lisabetta shrugged a shoulder. "I was but a little girl, monsieur—and a stray-relation at best. Surely, Josephine's own children would be more likely to know of the treasure's whereabouts than I would?

The Empress did wear the sapphire *parure* for all to see." Some of Josephine's more famous gems were rumored to have originated from the St. Alban's treasure-trove.

But her companion did not seem persuaded, and persisted, "Would your sister have any knowledge? She is older than you, and may remember more."

A bit tartly, Lisabetta retorted, "I know not what Eugenie knows, nor what she doesn't."

Thoughtfully, he added, "No one seems to know what has happened to her."

"I imagine she has finally crossed the wrong person, monsieur, and has suffered her just desserts."

He twisted his lips. "There is no love lost, between you."

"I do not clutter my mind with thoughts of Eugenie, monsieur."

Then I hope you will clutter it with thoughts of me, instead. I have come here, today, because I am willing to offer you my protection."

Wary, Lisabetta drew her brows down. "Why does the British government seek to intervene in this matter?"

"No—you misunderstand. I am offering my hand in marriage."

CHAPTER 2

Lisabetta stared at him in abject surprise. "*Marry* you?"

With a small smile, he bowed his head. "I astonish you."

She laughed. "You do indeed. And I can be forgiven for thinking that you are only after my treasure, monsieur."

"There would be less chance of anyone's wresting it from you, certainly."

This, of course, was true; under Napoleonic law, a wife's property became her husband's upon marriage, which was why the sudden loss of Josephine's protection could have grave consequences for Lisabetta; with a treasure-trove at stake, the authorities could easily turn a blind eye to any forced marriage.

In all admiration, she offered, "This is a very good gambit, I think. One of your best."

But he only shook his head. "No—it is not a

gambit, Lisabetta; I believe we would deal very well together. I am not your first choice and you are not mine, but we understand each other very well, I think."

Bemused, she couldn't help but ask, "You would trust me?"

"No, but you wouldn't trust me, either."

She had to laugh. "This is of all things true."

"It would solve all pressing problems. You would be protected, and I would gain access to the St. Alban's treasure." He paused, and then glanced at her from under his brows. "If it exists."

Holding up her palms, she readily replied, "You must trust me in this one thing, monsieur. I do not know where it is."

"I will hold my own opinion on that subject."

Making a show of concern, she offered, "Then I fear you would be disappointed in your bargain. You would soon resent our marriage, if I do not bring the fabulous dowry you seek."

"It may be just as useful," he pointed out practically, "to allow the other players to believe that England has secured it, whether or not she actually has."

This was undoubtedly true, and she could see his point. The various countries who'd successfully defeated Napoleon were now vying to seize their own power in the post-war chaos, with France, Prussia, England and Russia all meeting together in Vienna to divide-up Napoleon's former conquests. Behind the guise of diplomacy, the former allies were attempting to bribe, coerce or double-cross all the others so as to come out on top; the negotiations may have been more peaceful than open warfare, but they were just as ruthless. In light of this, the rumor that England had seized control of the St. Alban's treasure would only fortify that country's already strong position.

Whilst she was silent for a moment, he added, "And aside from your dowry, there would be an additional benefit to our alliance; if I could convince you to hold faith with England, I believe that you would be a very valuable asset."

Thoughtfully, she gazed at him without replying. Since she'd acted as an operative during the past few years—sometimes with England, and sometimes against her—a casual observer might come to the conclusion that she was loyal to whoever paid her the most money. It was a fair assessment, even though it was erroneous; she was, in fact, very loyal—but few people knew who held her allegiance.

Gauging her silence, he continued, "At the risk of being indelicate, I will point out that it is very unlikely you could steal Droughm away from his wife."

But Lisabetta immediately corrected him, "Fah—I do not look to steal Droughm away from his wife—I like her too much. She would have made a far better sister to me than Eugenie."

"Your pardon," he said.

"On the other hand, I could try to steal Seigneur

de Gilles away from his wife," she added thoughtfully. "That would be a triumph, indeed."

He smiled dryly. "A worthy aspiration, but alas—also unlikely."

With a tilt of her head, she conceded, "It does appear that all my best options have married."

"All the more reason to marry me, then. And—at the risk of being indelicate yet again—you are of an age where you might seriously think of a home, and children."

"*De vrai*, I am not getting any younger," she agreed. "But I thought you hoped I would work for England?"

He shrugged. "You may do both, or you may do neither; I will have gained my object, as well as an intelligent wife with an admirable mind."

Curious, she asked, "Do *you* seek a home, and children?"

"I do, if it means my country will survive the next war."

There was a small silence, whilst she thought this over. "How did you know I was here?"

"It is my business to know such things."

She raised her brows. "You have operatives in this place, too?"

Politely, he bowed his head. "I would rather not disclose my methods."

In a teasing tone, she observed, "It is a wonder that that you can find me, yet you cannot find the St. Alban's treasure."

Gallantly, he replied, "Only one is the greater treasure."

But she only observed with a touch of humor, "The truth of the matter is that you were prevented from going after the treasure whilst Josephine was alive—and it must have been of all things annoying, when the diplomats told someone such as you that you could not do whatsoever you wished."

"In this, we are very similar."

With a chuckle, she couldn't help but agree. "Yes, we are very similar. Which—in the end—may not be so very conducive for a marriage, *mon ami*. Perhaps you should go offer your hand to Eugenie; she may know more than I do about your elusive treasure."

His interest sharpened. "Perhaps I would, if only I could find her. Where is she, can you guess?"

"No. I do not know if she yet lives, but if she does, I can only hope that she stays as far away from me as possible."

He cocked his head. "Eugenie would be very unhappy to hear that we have wed."

She laughed. "Oh—you tempt me sorely, monsieur."

He rose, and she followed suit. "You will consider my offer, please. As I said, you are now at risk."

"You honor me, monsieur," she replied, teasing him with a demure tone.

He glanced over at her as he pulled on his gloves. "We would have many tales to tell our children, Lisabetta."

"If we survived long enough," she pointed out in a practical manner.

"There is that." He took her hand, and bowed over it formally. "*Au revoir*, mademoiselle."

Dipping a curtesy, she replied, "*Au revoir*, monsieur."

CHAPTER 3

⚜

*A*fter the Englishman closed the door behind him, Lisabetta stood in the visitor's parlor for a few moments in silence. The first player plays his card, she thought; and the gambit begins.

Without waiting for her proctor, she lifted her woolen cloak from the array of hooks near the door and swung it 'round her shoulders, as she walked through the vestibule to the Abbey's massive front doors. Smiling at the porter who hurried over to open for her, she then stepped outside into the weak sunlight, and began walking along the perimeter path that led to the kitchen garden—around the back of the massive stone building. The Abbey commanded an impressive view of the Rhine River from its perch high on the cliff, and she admired the reflection of the sunlight on the rippling water—just as she'd done so many times before. Such a beautiful place, she thought; a shame, that I am well-sick of it.

As could be anticipated, she was soon joined by

Dom Julian, who fell into step beside her. "What did he say to you?"

The good Abbot seemed a bit agitated, beneath his smooth exterior, and she hid a smile. "I would be very much surprised if you were not eavesdropping, *mon Abbé*."

He would not admit to this, of course, but instead replied, "His appearance here is very concerning, Lisabetta; you should not make light."

"Fah—it seems you look for any excuse to scold me, today," she replied easily.

There were a few steps of silence, and then—in a more conciliatory tone—he offered, "I beg your pardon. I will admit that I am unsettled by these events."

"And with good cause," she agreed, and glanced up so that he knew she was not annoyed with him. "It is very unsettling that he knows I am here. Is it possible that he has an operative, planted within your walls?"

"He does seem very well-informed," her companion admitted.

"Keep a sharp eye on the vendors who come to the gates," she suggested. "What of the man who delivered your lenses, yesterday?"

But he shook his head, slightly. "I am certain that he can be trusted."

Curious, she glanced at him. "Is he a Knight?"

"I would rather not say."

This, because those who ran the Abbey were actually a secret chapter of the Knights of Malta, an ancient Church Order that had been founded to honor St. John the Apostle. The Knights of Malta had absorbed what was left of the Knights Templar when that Order had been forcibly disbanded, but in the present century it was suffering its own trials; Napoleon had expelled the Knights from the Island of Malta, and—due to the Emperor's continued persecution of the Catholic Church—the Order had been forced out of Europe to St. Petersburg, where it now existed at the mercy of the Tsar of Russia.

The ancient Order consisted of men—some who were priests, and some who were not—who worked to further the aims of the Church; in particular, the Order was steadfast in fighting slavery and working to improve medical treatment for the poor.

Fairly, she acknowledged, "I suppose I cannot blame you for withholding information—matters being as they are. The fewer of your secrets I know, the better."

"I must think of your own safety, too, Lisabetta; these are treacherous times."

"*De vrai*—almost more treacherous than the war itself. Your Order is caught between England and Russia—and even the Holy Mother Church, who has to make concessions to survive. We can only hope that Monsieur Tallyrand holds faith, and does not consider how useful the Abbey's lands could be for him; he is ever in need of bribes."

"*Deo volente*," her companion replied in a grave tone.

Lisabetta had served the notorious Tallyrand in

the past—coincidentally, as part of a negotiation concerning this very Abbey. Tallyrand was a powerful political figure who'd had something of a checkered career—first serving the instigators of the French Revolution, then turning around and serving Napoleon as one of his trusted ministers, and then turning around once again to represent the newly-restored French King in the current peace negotiations.

Originally a Catholic priest, Tallyrand was known for his intrigues and wiles—as was ably demonstrated by the fact that none of the adverse political factions he'd served had tried to throw him into prison, during his long and rather questionable career. Indeed, his political survival was a testament to his ability to curry favor—often through outright bribery or blackmail—and he was known to be ruthless in taking any advantage that he could.

In fact, Tallyrand's duplicity was the very reason that the Knights of Malta had managed to maintain Beaulieu Abbey. During Napoleon's reign, much of the rich Rhineland had been conscripted by the French Emperor and in that process, many German princelings had been ousted from their estates. To placate the German princes, Tallyrand had offered them premiere properties along the Rhine River—properties that were formerly owned by the Catholic Church. The Abbey had been targeted for just such a fate, but then Tallyrand had abruptly changed his mind, and decided to allow the Abbey to become a beggar's hostel, instead. And—in an interesting coincidence—around that same time, Lisabetta had become Tallyrand's operative, traveling the world to monitor those persons who might pose a threat to the wily diplomat.

Tallyrand would be very surprised, of course, to learn that Lisabetta had double-crossed him on more than one occasion, depending on where her own interests lay. Or perhaps he wouldn't be surprised; after all, someone like Tallyrand would be the first to appreciate double-dealing.

Her mention of Tallyrand—which brought to mind the sacrifices she'd made to preserve the Abbey—seemed to provoke a more conciliatory attitude in her companion, and he offered, "If I was unkind, earlier—"

"Fah—I deserved a scolding, and it is already forgotten," she assured him. "I will think of another plan. Have you had the chance to test-out your new lenses?"

For a moment, he seemed reluctant to allow her to change the topic, but then he replied, "Tomorrow morning. Morning light is always best."

She nodded. The Abbot of Beaulieu was something of an amateur scientist, and at present, he was conducting different experiments in an attempt to create a stronger microscope. He ascribed to the revolutionary new theory that every substance on earth was made up of tiny cells, and that—indeed—unhealthy strains of these cells were the cause of human disease. This novel view was gradually taking the place of the previously accepted knowledge—that illnesses were caused by an unbalance of humors in the body.

However, much of the problem in verifying this new "cell theory" stemmed from the fact that microscopes could not look beyond a certain magnification without brighter light—ambient light needed to be amplified, somehow. Therefore, Julian was experimenting with lenses he'd ordered from an eyeglass-maker, setting the lenses at different distances to gauge how best to focus a brighter light on the materials he was observing.

Lisabetta was not of a scientific bent, but she could respect his work—which was mostly done in secret, being as questions might be raised if the Director of a beggar's hostel were found to be engaged in scientific experimentation, not to mention that the Church itself was sometimes ambivalent on the subject of scientific research. Indeed, the Church would be very surprised to discover that the chickens in the Abbey's barnyard often served as experimental subjects, being as Julian would inject their eggs with various concoctions and watch the emerging results under his microscope.

She knit her brows thoughtfully. "Perhaps the Abbey has been infiltrated by one of the guests. Can you think of any who might be working for the Englishman?"

"Two new guests this week," he replied. "One is in the infirmary."

When the Knights had acquired the Abbey, its former armory had been transformed into an infirmary so as to care for the destitute sick, and it was all rather ironic in that a former armory had now become a place of healing.

Julian continued, "The new patient claims to be sickening, but the Hospitaller is not certain that his concerns are legitimate. On the other hand, we have no indication that he is anything other than what he seems—he has done nothing to invoke suspicion, and seems disinclined to rise from his bed."

This was always a concern, in that—whilst a beggar's hostel served as an excellent way-station for the Knights' own operatives, who would inform Dom Julian of any new developments on the Continent—it also meant that the Abbey must welcome strangers whose motives might be less pure.

Lisabetta glanced at him. "Shall I make this sick man's acquaintance?"

He bowed his head. "If you would."

As part of her calling, Lisabetta was very adept at ferreting-out information; she was charming and beautiful, and men tended to lose their bearings when they were in the presence of a woman who was charming and beautiful. Or most men, at least; there was a notable exception who walked beside her.

With a knit brow, she asked, "Has the new patient shown any interest in Sebastian?"

"Not that I am aware. I am told he has asked no questions."

With some relief, she nodded. "Good. How does Sebastian, this morning?"

His voice softened. "As well as can be expected. He is constantly in my prayers."

"I will visit him today," she decided. "He should hear the news about Josephine firsthand."

But her companion cautioned, "Is that wise? The Englishman may be seeking-out Sebastian; I cannot like his prompt appearance, immediately after Josephine's death. You must be very careful, Lisabetta."

Teasing, she replied, "You know better than most that I am never careful, *mon Abbé.*"

But he was not to be teased on the subject, and replied a bit gravely, "It is not the usual circumstance, though. Your protectress is dead, and she has died just as the various factions from the war are desperate for funding. It is an unhappy coincidence."

Appreciating his concern, she soothed, "I am only teasing you, Julian—I will be very careful, my promise. I need only find a worthy husband to marry my treasure, and all will be well." This was self-evident; the best and fastest way to secure the treasure would be for Lisabetta to marry—and not just any husband, but one who held enough power to protect his newfound riches from the other powerful players.

With a nod, the Abbot clasped his hands behind his back. "Yes—that does seem the best solution. To this end, I will arrange for another masquerade ball, and quickly. I will admit I am alarmed that the English contingent has shown itself so boldly."

"Perhaps the Englishman simply wishes to marry me," she teased. "Is it so unthinkable?"

But it seemed that her companion was unwilling to make light about this particular subject, and warned, "The Englishman will not hesitate to apply whatever pressure he can, Lisabetta—there is little he would not do to put his hands on the treasure-trove. We must move to protect it—and you—with whatever counter-measures we can."

"Then I do not object to another masquerade ball," she replied lightly. "I very much enjoyed the last one."

With a touch of humor, he observed, "We will hope to avoid another melee."

"Not on my account, please; there is nothing like a melee, to sort-out the wheat from the chaff. Any husband of mine should be able to handle himself in a melee—it should be a prerequisite."

"Nevertheless," he advised in a dry tone, "it would be best to make arrangements for your marriage as quietly as possible—and as quickly; it would quash any notion that your fortune could be seized by force."

"As you wish. It will be very diverting, to see who shows their colors."

"I believe there has already been talk of putting forth the Baron Covairre." He glanced at her, weighing her reaction.

"Covairre would agree to marry me?" she asked in all surprise. "*Tiens*, the King of France must be applying prodigious pressure, if Covairre is willing to marry a baseborn bride—not to mention that I am no innocent maiden."

"I imagine the King thinks—and rightly—that your husband must have enough standing to offer solid protection, or else there is little point to your marriage. He has to be someone who can check both England and Russia, and because Corvairre is the one of the King's closest ministers, he would serve that purpose."

She nodded thoughtfully. "Yes—although the irony is sharp; Covairre's late wife thought me a strumpet, and lifted her skirts away whenever she passed by."

"She had no claim to higher morals," he retorted, nettled.

"Oh-ho," she teased, laughing. "Could that be a touch of spite I hear from you, *mon Abbé*? I am amazed."

Smiling slightly, he demurred, "Pray forget I said."

"Not likely—I appreciate your coming to my defense, even if it is a bit misguided. The woman is dead, after all."

"*Requiescat in pace*," he replied solemnly, and she laughed again.

CHAPTER 4

Later that afternoon, Lisabetta went about her rounds in the Abbey's infirmary, visiting with the men who were recovering from their illnesses. The large room was somewhat incongruous in that it had once been a castle armory, and still sported rows of medieval weapons racked upon the walls—crossbows and swords and other brutal weapons from wars fought long, long ago.

The infirmary was on the Abbey's ground floor, and adjacent to the entry to the main tower, as befit an armory—only nowadays, instead of armored soldiers there were patients arrayed in the row of cots pushed against the wall. The large room also had several smaller antechambers attached to it, to house those patients who were considered infectious, or those who were dying and would thus appreciate some peace.

Lisabetta's proctor settled into his chair by the door whilst she began to make her rounds, visiting with each patient one-by-one. Some were legitimate patients from the local area, but there were a few who were travelers with a purpose, Knights staying at the infirmary for several days to pass along information to the Order, and taking information with them to be passed along in turn. In these uncertain times, having an up-to-date communications network was essential; in particular, the Order needed to keep a close watch on the Congress that was ongoing in Vienna, because several of the factions were looking to curtail the Church's power—Protestant England first amongst them. And because England wielded the power to set the course of the Congress, this constituted a grave threat to the Order—therefore careful monitoring was essential. It was yet another reason that the Abbot was left uneasy by the grey-eyed man's unexpected appearance on his doorstep; his Order was already at the mercy of the Russian Tsar, and the Russian Tsar was necessarily having to curry favor with England—everyone was.

Lisabetta moved amongst the patients—wearing a plain kerchief and apron—inquiring if she could write letters home for the sick men. For those who were legitimate patients, hopefully there were relatives who could be contacted since the hostel was in the practical business of trying to reunite the destitute sick with their families. But those who were false patients would give Lisabetta information under the guise of dictating a letter—usually using code words—to be passed along to Dom Julian, who would then distill what information should be passed along to the various Knights in their network. Due to the ongoing negotiations in Vienna, there'd been a steady influx of these types of patients for the past few weeks, and today was no exception.

Unhurriedly, Lisabetta made her rounds, and then came to the last patient—the one that Dom Julian had mentioned as a potential infiltrator. He was a man named Hahn, who hailed from India.

"*Bon jour*," she greeted him. "Do you speak French?"

"I prefer to speak Malayalam," he volunteered with a gleam.

She gave him a look. "Perhaps English, instead."

"My French is not so good," he admitted in English.

"You must remedy that," she advised, as she pretended to make a note. "French is the language of diplomacy."

"Yes; they all sound like bleating sheep, talking through their noses."

"Nevertheless," she replied calmly, and made another pretend-note.

"I have been told much about you," he observed boldly. "And it is true; you are very beautiful. I am surprised you have no husband."

"I am hoping that situation will be remedied very soon," she replied, unruffled.

With a sly gleam, he ventured, "Have you a dowry? Perhaps that is the problem."

She lifted her gaze to his, a warning contained

therein. "Do not be impertinent."

He shrugged. "I am so very bored. I must amuse myself somehow."

"Not for the next few weeks," she warned. "You are sick, and must rest."

"Oh—yes, I must rest; I am sick," he remembered, and coughed for dramatic effect.

She paused her pen for a moment, and glanced at him from under her lashes. "It would pay to be more cautious," she advised. "I do not think you have been long in the game, and it is a dangerous one."

"It is a very confusing game," he admitted. "No one is what they seem."

"I have made the acquaintance of both Kings and beggars," Lisabetta replied, "and I will agree with you. But you would do well to listen to my advice, lest you find yourself trussed in a barrel at the bottom of the Rhine."

He stared at her. "You alarm me."

"When much is at stake, much will be risked. Remember your assignment, and do not be distracted."

He quirked his mouth. "I have little choice; you are the only woman on the premises."

"Women make men weak," she cautioned. "Any time an alluring woman shows an interest in you, you should be wary of her motives."

He drew his brows down. "I think you insult me."

"Perhaps," she acknowledged, and made another note. "Keep your mind on your coming reward, instead."

"I will," he promised, and shifted down in the bed, so as to draw the coverlet over his head. "Good night."

"It is but afternoon," Lisabetta pointed out.

"It hardly matters," the muffled voice complained. "I am so very bored."

With a graceful movement, Lisabetta then rose to signal to the proctor that she would visit Sebastian, a patient who'd been kept isolated in one of the adjacent antechambers due to the fact that his mysterious illness was believed contagious. He'd been at the Abbey's infirmary for some months, now, and at first it was believed that he suffered from smallpox, and so he'd been kept in strict isolation. This theory had to be discarded, however, when he failed to either recover or succumb; instead, his illness lingered, with new pustules making an appearance every now and then, and the patient continuing weak and bedridden.

Careful strictures had been put in place to protect the other patients, with only the Hospitaller and Dom Julian allowed to enter the sickroom—along with Lisabetta, on rare occasions; because the nature of the illness was unknown, it paid to be careful.

Lisabetta closed the door behind her, and then turned to review the small, still figure in the bed—the patient's pale face suddenly breaking into a warm smile.

"Good afternoon, dearest," the patient said softly.

"Good afternoon, Eugenie," Lisabetta replied.

CHAPTER 5

Lisabetta considered the frail figure of her sister, and decided she seemed no worse than the week before. After drawing up a stool, she sat and clasped the patient's hand. "How are you feeling today, my darling?"

"Much better," Eugenie replied, even though this was always her answer, no matter the reality. She was suffering from the wasting disease, and—in truth—she should have died long before now, save that Dom Julian was compiling all the knowledge he'd ever acquired so as to treat her illness—and was doing his own bit of unsanctioned experimentation, besides.

Like her sister, Eugenie had served as an operative in the last war, only her role tended to be more behind-the-scenes, and therefore had been less varied—and less dangerous—than Lisabetta's. She was another beauty, with hair as fair as Lisabetta's was dark—indeed, sometimes Lisabetta wondered if their mother had played her lover false; such things weren't unheard of, in the circles that the woman had traveled.

With a smile, Lisabetta offered, "I have interesting news—this morning I received an offer of marriage from the Englishman."

Eugenie stared at her in astonishment. "It is a trick."

"Of course, it is—give me a thimbleful of credit, dearest."

But Eugenie had seized upon the most alarming aspect of this news. "How did he know you were here?"

"He has eyes and ears everywhere, I am afraid. And the timing is not a surprise." She paused. "Josephine has died."

Eugenie's expression turned grave, as she searched her sister's eyes. "Has she? How did it come about?"

"An illness, apparently. Although she was not known to be sickening."

Eugenie's gaze shifted to the wall, as she considered this. "These are dangerous times."

"Yes. But to be fair, I have heard no rumors that it was deliberate."

Making a sound of sympathy, the other young woman shook her head sadly. "The poor Emperor. No matter that he married another; it was always Josephine who held his heart."

"He will grieve, there is no doubt. But more importantly, he thirsts for funding."

Bringing her gaze back to meet Lisabetta's, her

sister cautioned, "Oh—oh yes; small wonder the Englishman seeks your hand. You must be very careful, Betta."

But Lisabetta only chuckled. "*Tiens*—you sound like Dom Julian, Genie. You know better than most that I am never careful." She paused, a smile playing around her lips. "As a matter of fact, he quarreled with me today—Dom Julian did."

Eugenie raised her pale brows in surprise. "He *quarreled* with you??

Lisabetta nodded. "Scolded me, up one side and down the other."

"Betta," Eugenie asked in an ominous tone. "What have you done?"

"I asked him to marry me."

Eugenie stared for an astonished moment, and then laughed aloud, the sound very welcome to her sister's ears. "Oh—did you, indeed?"

"I did. I told him it would be the best way to secure the treasure, now that Josephine can no longer cast her mantle of protection over us."

Still very much amused, Eugenie scolded gently, "Do not tease the poor man, Betta—he is so dedicated."

"Well, I have to marry someone, and soon. As a matter of fact, he's planning another masquerade ball."

A spark of interest flared in Eugenie's eyes. "Will Charles attend?"

She referred to the notorious Tallyrand, for whom she'd once been fond, and Lisabetta replied gently, "I doubt it, dearest—he has not left the Congress since it began. The old rogue must stay vigilant there, and keep his fingers in many pies."

With a small sigh, Eugenie nodded. "It is just as well—I'd rather he remembered me as I was, and not as I am. And it would be best not to bring any attention to Angelique."

Although the last words were said in an even tone, Lisabetta immediately clasped both her hands around her sister's. "Shall I bring her to the yard again, to feed the chickens? You can watch her from the window."

"No, Betta—truly, I am not grieved. Better that she stays where she is happy; better she knows nothing of her parents."

"She is thriving," Lisabetta assured her. "And Dom Julian will arrange for a tutor, next year when she turns school-age." With some emphasis, she added, "You mustn't worry, dearest; between the two of us, we will see that Angelique has an honorable future."

"A better aunt cannot be imagined," Eugenie pronounced softly.

"She is my very own stray-relation," Lisabetta explained with a smile. "And so, I am determined to smooth her path."

Since she couldn't stay long, Lisabetta rose to plump the pillows behind the other young woman's head and advised, "Dom Julian tells me that you are improving, Eugenie. By summer, we will be sitting on the banks of the Rhine and watching the sailboats."

"I like that plan," her sister said softly. Unspoken was the unfortunate fact that she was unlikely to survive that long.

CHAPTER 6

It was a steep, winding road from the Abbey to the village below, and it made for an enjoyable walk, when the weather was cooperating. Lisabetta breathed in the scent of the dense trees as she made her way down to the Beaulieu village, and contemplated the tasks before her, now that the gambit had been set in motion. It was important to stay flexible; she'd learned from long experience that any plan should only be considered a starting point, and that events had a way of straying out of control.

Hopefully, once her tasks in the village were completed she'd find a cart headed back up to the Abbey, and could beg for a lift—although she'd walked this steep hill many a time, even as a child, when the Abbey had seemed like a fairy-tale castle perched atop its crest. A fairy-tale castle, right down to the Knights who'd acted swiftly to hide them—her mother and the two little girls, along with the two large barrels that were ostensibly filled with fish oil.

Dom Nicolas had been the Abbott back then, with Julian still a stripling in his teens when their flatboat had landed in the middle of the night, the huddled passengers cold and thoroughly frightened. Julian had then carried Lisabetta on his back up the hill—whispering encouraging words to the traumatized little girl, even as he was supposed to stay silent. At that time, the Abbey was still a monastery, but in truth it was a base for the Knights of Malta, who'd covertly settled in several key locations along the Rhine. Lisabetta's father was a cousin to Dom Nicolas, and so the Abbot had willingly arranged for sanctuary; the fact that the refugees brought a priceless treasure along with them had no doubt factored favorably into this decision.

Lisabetta had only vague and unformed memories of that night; the darkness of the river because they dared not light a lantern, her pretty mother weeping because her lover had been hauled off to the notorious Parisian prison, and Eugenie doing her best to comfort the rather frivolous woman, who was in no way prepared to be a desperate refugee. The only clear memory that stood out, in fact, was that of being carried on the back of a kindly, strong young man who'd assured her in a steady voice that all would be well.

It was a novelty for the young Lisabetta; their father had been an indistinct figure in their lives, in that his illegitimate children were not nearly as important as his favorite mistress—not to mention he'd more than a few other mistresses and children, besides. Her father would smile and speak kindly when he saw the little girls, but his gaze always seemed to be straying elsewhere; he'd another family, her mother had explained, and so he could not spare them much of his time. They were his stray-relations; never first in mind, and of far less value than his legitimate family.

And so, little Lisabetta had listened to Julian's encouraging words and had given over her allegiance to him without a moment's hesitation; an allegiance that would last—steadfast and secure—for her entire life, despite anything that would happen, and anything that could possibly come to be. There was an unshakable bond between them—she knew, in her heart of hearts, that he felt it too, but due to his calling it was nothing she could ever act upon; she loved him too much to try to breach the honor that he wore around him like a shield.

Until, of course, everything had changed, and she'd caught a tiny glimpse of the blazing happiness that might be brought about if only she could plan it —oh, so carefully. And now, all careful plans had been suddenly accelerated by the Empress's death; in a strange way, her death had been a boon—leave it to Josephine, to be as helpful in death as she had been in life.

Hard on this thought, Lisabetta turned from the main road to walk down a path toward a merchant's house that was located just outside the village, shifting her basket to the other hip so that she could knock on the door. The basket was heavy, as it always was when she came to visit; much heavier than it would be when she left.

"Mademoiselle Lisabetta," Sophie greeted her as she opened the door. "How good to see you again. Do you make a lengthy visit at the Abbey, this time?"

"I imagine I will be away again and soon, unfortunately. Josephine has died—have you heard?"

The woman nodded. "I have. What does it mean for us?"

"Nothing for you," Lisabetta assured her. "But as for me, I will have to find another protector, and quickly."

"These times," Sophie replied with all sympathy. "God is testing us."

"More like He has washed his hands," Lisabetta replied in a dry tone. "I have brought fresh eggs—let me bring Angelique her new dolls."

With an exclamation of gratitude, Sophie held the basket whilst Lisabetta lifted several wooden dolls from within. "Many thanks, mademoiselle—join us for luncheon, and I will make an omelet."

"Thank you, but I cannot stay long, I'm afraid—I have errands to run. Leave a few eggs in the basket, if you would; I will go barter them at the fishmonger's."

She then carried the dolls into the parlor, where an elderly man sat on a comfortable chair near the windows, his feet propped up on a stool. The room's other occupant was a little girl of four years, who sat on the rug as she played with an elaborate dollhouse.

Upon sighting Lisabetta, the man smiled, his face creased with wrinkles. "Mademoiselle Betta."

The little girl looked up with a shy smile, which turned into excitement as she caught sight of the new dolls. "*Merci*, Mam'selle Betta," she exclaimed, and leapt up to accept them happily. "Will you play with me?"

"In a moment, Angelique." Lisabetta walked over to the older man, bending to take his hand with great fondness. "*Bon jour* Georges, you old rogue; how are you?"

Pleased, he covered her hand with his own. "I do well, mademoiselle."

"I have brought more dolls—we never seem to have enough," she teased.

The older man bowed his head, but made no reply. In truth, he crafted the wooden dolls himself, and saw them secretly delivered to the Abbey. Each contained a hollowed-out cavity so as to smuggle jewels and gold coins back to his household—jewels and coins which were then smuggled on to other destinations.

She continued, "I have brought fresh eggs, but the chickens aren't half as useful as they used to be. It may be time to wring their miserable little necks."

Again, the older man bowed his head but made no reply.

Satisfied, Lisabetta walked over to join Angelique on the rug. Georges had been the manservant who'd escorted them up the Rhine on that fateful night, so long ago—apparently he was the only man their father could trust to complete the task without seizing the treasure for himself. As a reward for his loyalty, Dom Nicolas had arranged for Georges to have a trading contract with the Abbey, so that the former servant would become a merchant of some means. The man had prospered in this role for nearly twenty years, and then, when Eugenie had given birth to Angelique, he'd been the natural choice to take the baby quietly into his household. To this end, he'd married Sophie, a widow from the village who had no children of her own.

Sophie was an attractive woman with ample curves—many years younger than Georges—and she was delighted with her new role as a village *bourgeoise*. She didn't mind raising Angelique, especially since this meant she'd have plenty of spending money to match her new status—Georges was very generous with his new family.

But Georges had not chosen well, unfortunately, and Lisabetta had witnessed this phenomenon many a time; the ampler the curves, the less likely it was that the man would consider the character of the woman he'd chosen.

And, since this type of woman never tended to be content, it was not much of a surprise that Sophie had been secretly approached by Tallyrand, and bribed to make monthly reports to the minister about the doings in her household.

Small blame to Tallyrand, Lisabetta reflected

fairly; very few knew about the child he'd fathered upon one of Josephine's wards, and if anyone discovered this very interesting information, the tables would be turned, and Tallyrand would be the one who was being blackmailed for a change. In his heyday, he wouldn't have much cared—he'd been Napoleon's right hand, and no one would have dared to make an enemy of him. But now—now he was not nearly so powerful, and was having to step lively to maintain his position. It was a very helpful turn of events, all in all.

With a smile, Lisabetta settled on the floor beside Angelique, inquiring after her dolls and unable to resist taking one of the girl's flaxen curls between her fingers—her hair was so like Eugenie's, before the illness had taken its toll. "A new dollhouse, and larger than the last. Did Monsieur Georges make it?"

"Yes, Mam'selle; do you see? It has a parlor, just like ours—even with the hearth."

"Is there a secret passage? The best kind of houses have a secret passage or two—you never know when you might have to escape." Lisabetta, from many a past experience, knew of which she spoke.

"I don't think so," the girl said doubtfully. She then lowered her voice and disclosed, "There is no stairway. I think Monsieur Georges forgot to make a stairway."

But Lisabetta was not at all dismayed by this. "It would take up too much room, so it is better not to have one. Instead, you may pretend they can fly from one level to the next." She demonstrated this, lifting one of the dolls to the second level. "Sometimes you must pretend things. On the other hand, sometimes you build your stairway, step by step."

Her little brow knit, Angelique regarded her aunt doubtfully. "I don't know how to build a stairway."

"Then I will teach you, dearest. How would you like to go up to the Abbey and feed the chickens again?"

"Yes, please," the child said immediately. And then—with a touch of hesitation—she added, "You won't let them crowd 'round me again?"

"No—we will have you stand on a stool, this time, and all will be well." She paused, and ran a gentle hand over the girl's curls. "My promise on it."

CHAPTER 7

⚜

Lisabetta's next task was to visit the fishmonger's, to trade her remaining eggs for fillets if they'd anything fresh. The fishmonger was a longtime acquaintance, and she greeted him warmly. "Antoine; as handsome as ever."

The big, beefy man chuckled. "I was wondering if you'd turn up, mademoiselle." With a full measure of self-importance, he lowered his voice. "Josephine has died; have you heard?"

"I have," she replied solemnly, thinking it amusing that the man would think he'd have heard before she did.

Her companion shook his head sadly. "The poor Emperor; so many trials to endure."

"We must never lose hope, *mon ami*," Lisabetta reminded him, a gentle hand on his arm. Antoine was a staunch Napoleon loyalist, and had readily agreed to be a part of Tallyrand's network of spies along the Rhine—the river being a well-used conduit for communication. It was rather unfortunate that Antoine was somewhat naïve, and thus was unaware that Tallyrand's goals did not necessarily match Napoleon's—as could be easily demonstrated by the fact that the wily minister had plotted with the Russian Tsar behind Napoleon's back, or that he was now negotiating on behalf of the new French King at the Congress. Truly, it made one's head spin, and the poor fishmonger could hardly be blamed for failing to keep up; allegiances were shifting with every passing moment, as all the players from the last war were frantically trying to hedge their bets and survive. The diplomats may be civil in Vienna, but behind the scenes it was an all-out scramble to maintain scraps of power, with double-dealings and betrayals being the order of the day.

Antoine, however, was content in his belief that he nobly served his Emperor by making reports to Tallyrand, and he looked upon Lisabetta as a fellow-traveler who was likewise loyal—not to mention that he was somewhat in awe of her, since she could be considered someone within Napoleon's sacred circle.

He means well, Lisabetta thought charitably; and it is fortunate for me, since there is no one easier to manipulate than a man who is not very bright but means well.

Antoine had been tasked with keeping a close eye on the Abbey; Tallyrand may have arranged for the Knights to retain it, but in the end, he trusted no one —especially people who answered to God rather than to himself. And—since Dom Julian was well-aware that he was being thus scrutinized—on occasion he would give Lisabetta a bit of harmless information to pass along to Antoine, just so as to allow Tallyrand to believe he was being kept abreast of the Order's doings. It was amusing, truly, that bits and pieces of the St. Alban's treasure were regularly smuggled out right under Antoine's nose; the man tended to be more loyal than clever, and so it was a very helpful state of affairs.

After taking a furtive glance around them, the fishmonger asked, "How does the Director?"

"The Director is fiddling with his microscope, and hoping to cure the world's ills," Lisabetta replied, as she pressed a finger into a fillet so as to test its freshness. "But I've more important things on my mind—information that must be passed on to your master. The Englishman visited me yesterday—"

"The *Englishman* came *here*?" Antoine interrupted incredulously. "Why—I heard nothing of this."

"He moves like a shadow," Lisabetta replied, and diplomatically didn't mention that Antoine was easier to fool than most. "And even more alarming, he has proposed marriage to me."

Antoine stared at her, at a loss for words.

"*C'est vrai*," she affirmed. "It appears that the English are determined to lay hands upon the treasure-trove, but they must use discretion, and dare not wrest it outright. Monsieur Tallyrand should be made aware of this."

"Yes, yes," Antoine agreed gravely. "It is most distressing."

She lowered her voice, and took a quick glance around. "And I have even more troubling news, *mon ami*. I believe I saw Monsieur Darton here, just yesterday."

Again, her companion could barely control his surprise. "Darton *lives*?"

"Hush, hush," she warned, and thus prompted, he bent his head to wrap the filet in paper.

She continued in a low tone, "I saw only a glimpse, because he ducked out of sight. I pretended not to have noticed him."

With acute dismay, her companion asked, "Why would he be here?"

"That is a very good question, monsieur."

This news would indeed be alarming, if it were true. Darton had been Tallyrand's man before he'd mysteriously disappeared, and it was presumed that either someone had revealed his role as a spy—and the man was now dead—or that Darton had turned coat, and was now working to undermine his former master's plans—this latter option much more alarming than the first. To bring this point home, Lisabetta mused, "I wonder if he now works for the Englishman? It cannot be a coincidence, that they were both here at the same time."

In truth, Darton was dead—and by Lisabetta's own hand, as a matter of fact—but Tallyrand did not know this, and he would be duly alarmed by news of the man's reappearance at this crucial juncture, with so many interests competing for control. Due to Tallyrand's questionable activities behind-the-scenes,

Darton would have many secrets to sell, if he were so inclined.

Very much distressed by these revelations, the fishmonger handed Lisabetta her packet and muttered, "Monsieur Tallyrand will not like to hear of this."

Lisabetta made a sympathetic sound. "I will await instruction—another masquerade ball is being planned, and I will send word when the date is settled upon."

Antoine nodded. "Good. Will you be staying at the Abbey?"

"Yes—it is safest, I think."

He glanced around, thoroughly alarmed by what she'd revealed. "Do you have anything else to report?"

She made a show of considering his question for a moment. "Perhaps. A patient from India rests in the infirmary, but I think he is feigning his illness. He appeared on the same day that I caught a glimpse of Darton."

Antoine met her eyes and frowned. "*India* takes an interest?"

"India is England," she reminded him patiently.

He blew out a breath. "This is all very alarming."

"Everything is alarming, nowadays. I must go."

"Yes, yes; thank you, mademoiselle."

She left him, and then wandered slowly along the stalls, handling the occasional offering so that it wouldn't seem that her only object in coming here was to speak to Antoine. Meanwhile, she watched covertly as Antoine sauntered off in a casual fashion to speak to one of his fishermen who was working on the docks—Antoine's negligent posture belied by the intensity with which he bent to speak to the man, who continued to idly mend his nets.

Whilst she watched this interaction from beneath her lashes, the net-mender briefly raised his gaze to meet Lisabetta's—he knew she was watching them—and she quickly lowered her own gaze so as to avoid his mocking one. Jacques—unlike Antoine—was someone to be feared.

Antoine may have been Tallyrand's spy, but his questionable competence was illustrated by the fact he was completely unaware that the fisherman who answered to him was actually a spy for Napoleon—or more correctly, Napoleon's notorious spymaster, Rochon. Indeed, if it weren't so ominous it would be amusing; Antoine believed that Tallyrand served Napoleon still, but Jacques' presence here meant that Napoleon himself knew better, and that he was in turn monitoring everything that Antoine might pass along to Tallyrand.

And it also meant that Lisabetta was very careful to avoid Jacques—she hadn't survived this long by taking foolish chances. Rochon had—by far—the more ruthless and seasoned network of spies, and Rochon would bear a grudge against Lisabetta from a previous humiliation—he was not one to forgive and forget.

She'd warned Dom Julian about Jacques' true allegiances—although the Abbot tended to be very well-informed, and she wasn't certain whether he already knew this. It also meant they had to be very careful about which pieces of information were passed on to Antoine—whilst Tallyrand was aware that the Abbey continued to house the Knights of Malta, it was important that Napoleon not be made aware of this, in the event the Emperor rose to power again.

Which brought up another important point that did not bode well for Antoine; if Napoleon indeed regained power, the Emperor would bear a mighty grudge against Tallyrand, who'd turned coat and plotted against him. There would be serious reprisals for anyone who had taken Tallyrand's side in the meantime—even poor Antoine, who didn't realize his allegiance to Tallyrand was counter to Napoleon's interests. If the power in France shifted yet again, Jacques—the man's former assistant—would no doubt see to it that Antoine disappeared, never to be seen again.

Lisabetta had learned, long ago, not to become over-attached to anyone in the game, but she rather hoped the fishmonger wouldn't suffer for his naivete. It was often this way, though; the loyal faithful were sacrificed without a second thought, if their usefulness had come to an end, or if they were shown to be a weakness.

Although—come to think of it—it was a bit strange, that she'd heard no reports of Rochon and his doings, lately. Lisabetta always kept careful track of Napoleon's notorious spymaster so as to avoid crossing his path, but no one seemed to have heard any rumors of his whereabouts, for the past few months.

Brushing aside these troubling concerns, she turned back toward the main road; she'd had a very productive morning, and was well-satisfied with what had been accomplished.

CHAPTER 8

The following morning, Lisabetta tended to her early-morning chores with the chickens and then carried some of the eggs up to Dom Julian's laboratory at the top of the main tower, where the Abbot could be found catching the best sunlight for his experiments. The tower had been a defensive keep, back when the Abbey was a castle, and from its height there was an impressive view of the river and the surrounding hills. A shame, that a private visit with the man required a long climb up the winding stone stairway, but on the other hand it also meant that they were unlikely to be interrupted.

"Good morning, *mon Abbé*," she greeted him, setting the basket on a long wooden table. The room was well-organized—as fit its proprietor—with treatises piled in neat stacks and various tools hanging in their designated places. Dom Julian was seated at another, smaller table near the windows, bent over his microscope and making notes in a journal.

He glanced up at her greeting, but did not rise. "Where is your proctor, Lisabetta?"

"I did not enlist him, for fear he wouldn't be able to manage the stairs," she replied. "And in any event, my fabled dowry guarantees that I will soon be a married woman—the Baroness Corvairre, perhaps. It is a shame that we cannot witness the former Baroness's reaction to this turn of events."

He smiled slightly, but returned to his microscope. "Indeed."

She hid her satisfaction—the good Abbot's response to the mention of her marriage seemed equivocal at best—and changed the subject. "I told Sebastian the news about Josephine."

At this, he shifted on his stool to face her. "Yes; I saw him this morning, and he spoke of your visit."

"He seems no worse," she ventured.

Thoughtfully, he nodded. "I would agree; I am testing-out another's theory; a tincture derived from mustard plants seems to serve as a check on the illness—at least for a time."

"*Tiens*—that is very good news," she exclaimed, beyond willing to grasp at any thread of hope.

He cautioned, "As with any medication, the difficulty is in weighing the benefit against the adverse effects."

"You've done wonders, Julian. We both appreciate it."

He turned his gaze out the window. "If we could improve magnification, we could better study cellular regeneration. I think understanding regeneration is the key to curing this type of illness."

She nodded along, having little understanding of what he'd just said. "As long as the chickens' sacrifices will not have been made in vain."

Amused, he tilted his head. "I am afraid that I do not consider their feelings."

"Then I can relate to them, poor things. Tell me of the coming masquerade ball, so that I may hope for some entertainment."

"Next week, at the Palais," he advised. "And I would suggest that—until that time—you make no further trips into the village, Lisabetta. You risk yourself."

Stubbornly, she insisted, "I wanted to visit Angelique again—I was longing to see her. Could she come to feed the chickens again, so that Eugenie can watch through her window?"

He considered this for a moment, and then nodded. "You must be careful, though; if her relationship to you becomes known, she will be put at risk."

She nodded, since this was apparent—indeed, it was the very reason that the weakened Eugenie was being hidden away so carefully; the players in this game were ruthless, as they looked for any means to apply leverage—or even blackmail.

"What did you tell Antoine?"

"I asked if he knew of Josephine's death," she replied easily, not surprised that Julian knew of her morning's activities. "It would seem strange, if I didn't check-in with him about it, and he was very proud to report that he'd already heard."

"Good. Jacques was there?"

"He was. I resisted the impulse to ask him where Rochon was hiding himself."

But her companion did not seem amused by this sally, and instead fixed a thoughtful gaze upon her. "I am informed that Antoine showed great alarm when you spoke with him."

Inwardly cursing the village and its spies-upon-spies, she shrugged. "Antoine shows great alarm when the birds sing, Julian. I teased him about the Empress having been murdered by Napoleon's current wife, and he didn't realize, at first, that I was not serious."

He didn't reply immediately, and they regarded each other for a long moment, his gaze steady on hers. Slowly, he offered, "I am somewhat concerned, Lisabetta, that you visited the village this morning because you are running a gambit."

"Possibly," she hedged. She always had a hard time lying to him outright.

A gleam of amusement appeared in his eyes. "But you can't tell me what it is?"

Bluntly, she informed him, "No, I can't. You are too honorable, Julian; it is a failing, sometimes."

At this, he raised his dark brows. "That does not reassure me."

Carefully, she explained, "You are subject to constraints—and your Order is subject to constraints." She paused, trying to decide how much more she should say, and then decided she dared not say more. "And so, I cannot tell you," she concluded.

He nodded. "I see. Can you at least tell me of the new patient? I understand you spoke to him for some time."

"I think he is harmless," she assured him, inwardly annoyed that she felt so guilty at this additional untruth. "A merchant from India, looking to set-up a trade route along the Rhine."

This seemed to catch his interest, and he returned his gaze to the window. "Oh? Where, in India?"

"I've no idea. Why?"

"The physicians from the Kerala area are testing new treatments for the falling-sickness."

She smiled. "Trust you, to be distracted by such things whilst I am scrambling to survive. I thought you feared that the Englishman has planted a spy in our midst?"

He tilted his head, as he continued to gaze out the window. "I wonder if the Englishman has always known of the Order's work here, but was not over-concerned about it until now."

"It is possible," she agreed. "But—I suppose—now he is emboldened enough to confront you outright; Napoleon's a prisoner, Josephine's dead, and Tallyrand is not the *bête noire* he once was."

"Yes." He returned his gaze to hers. "The Englishman has handled you carefully in the past, Lisabetta, but now that there are rumors of Napoleon's return, he will be ruthless in securing his aims. The British need additional funding, and his proposal of marriage is, I fear, only the first salvo."

But she shrugged a negligent shoulder. "I do not fear him, Julian. We respect each other, the Englishman and I—even as we don't trust each other. I have done him some favors, as he has done me."

In gentle admonishment, he observed, "Surely any respect he has for you wouldn't supersede what he hopes to accomplish, Lisabetta—you are not so naïve."

She paused, and then tried to explain what she knew only by instinct. "It is hard for you to understand, perhaps—you are always so straightforward—but in my business, we tend to do favors for one another on the understanding that the favors may be returned, someday. We are all playing a deadly game, and our failures or successes will never be spoken of—*tiens*, our masters wouldn't even acknowledge us, if they were called upon to do so. And so, it is as though we belong to a—to a club, of sorts, and we respect one another, even as we have different allegiances. To the Englishman, an offer of marriage is a fair compromise; he would achieve his aims and I would not suffer for it. In return, he would hope that I would treat him just as fairly, if the situation ever arose."

But he was openly skeptical, and asked, "Surely you do not feel this way about Rochon?"

She smiled. "No—although I admit that I would very much enjoy hearing his offer of marriage."

A bit gravely, he persisted, "You make light, but I do not see much difference between them—Rochon and the Englishman. And both of them are enemies of the Church."

"A good point," she agreed mildly, even as she thought, oh-ho—it is very interesting that he is trying to harden me against the Englishman; in no universe would he be Rochon's equal in evildoing. In a light tone, she continued, "Such unbelievers—how dare they seek the St. Alban's treasure, so as to spread their heresy? Who does your Order fear more; godless Napoleon or the Protestant British?"

He took a breath, his chest rising and falling. "At this point, my Order seeks only to survive."

"Then I can sympathize with their concerns."

But this prompted him to offer with some emphasis, "My Order will protect you as it always has, Lisabetta—there is no need to rely on the Englishman. My oath on it."

He's a bit nettled, she decided, and I should soothe the poor man—no matter how much I am enjoying this promising display of jealousy. "And I am forever grateful, *mon Abbé*. Unfortunately, there is a great deal of money at stake, which does not bode well; I will remind you that you have already suggested I flee down the Rhine."

He made a sound of regret. "I will admit that the Englishman caught me by surprise. He won't again."

"I have every confidence that this is true," she agreed stoutly, and once again, hid a smile; the Abbot of Beaulieu may not know it, but there would be many more surprises to come.

CHAPTER 9

Lisabetta stepped closer to his table, and made an inquiring gesture toward the microscope. "Now that we are finished with inconsequential topics, tell me, if you will, what it is that you gaze upon."

"Cells from a mustard plant," Julian explained. "Come look, if you'd like."

Dutifully, she stepped forward and leaned to peer through the scope—wishing she'd thought to remove her apron beforehand, since her leaning posture would have exposed him to a tempting view.

With a small frown, she squinted at the strange little semi-transparent formations that he seemed to find so fascinating, and pretended an interest. She always pretended an interest in his experiments, and listened carefully to his explanations even though she didn't understand most of it. Nevertheless, she wanted to share in it—wanted to let him know that he could speak of such things to her; it was his passion, after all.

Well—one of his passions, anyway. The other one was revealed some years ago, on that terrible night when Rochon—Napoleon's spymaster—had decided it would be best to eliminate Lisabetta altogether, since she'd shown an alarming willingness to double-deal with the British.

Rochon had many operatives along this busy stretch of the river—Jacques being only one of them—and so he'd commissioned one of his thugs to stuff her into a barrel, bound and gagged, so as to summarily toss her into the Rhine to drown, thinking that no one would ever be the wiser; he was at the height of his powers, and did whatever he thought he could get away with.

Fortunately for her, Dom Julian had unearthed the plot, and even though he dared not challenge Rochon openly, he'd watched these events from the tree-line along the river, and then had raced downriver to dive in and haul the sinking barrel onto the riverbank.

Even now, as she recalled that feeling of helpless terror, Lisabetta suppressed a shudder—fah, but there was a bad memory. But something good had come of it, in that when Julian had frantically broken through the barrel-lid with the hilt of his knife, the expression on his face spoke volumes.

"*Deo Gratias, Deo Gratias,*" he'd muttered, as he drew the coughing and sobbing Lisabetta into his arms—holding her so tightly that she could barely catch her already-ragged breath. "Hush, Lisabetta—I have you," he'd soothed—much the same as he'd done that first time, when he'd carried her up the hill as a child.

The unguarded moment had passed, and—taking hold of himself—he was in the process of sawing through her bindings when the perpetrator came up from behind to attack him, furious at having being thwarted in his mission. Julian managed to throw off the man, and then—without a moment's hesitation or regret—he'd driven his knife straight into the other man's heart.

They'd then stood there, in the dim moonlight; Julian's chest heaving from his exertions as Lisabetta stared at the dead man, trying to pull together her scattered wits. "He must disappear," she whispered. "We will load him into the barrel, and he is the one who will sink to the bottom."

"He must be shriven, and buried properly," Julian had protested.

"Not if either one of us hopes to survive," she'd replied quietly.

After a moment's consideration, he'd nodded. "We must pray for him, then."

"I am not going to pray for him," she'd advised in a sharp tone.

"I will, then." And he'd knelt in the sand beside the dead assassin.

Taking a long breath, she reluctantly knelt beside him, and pretended to pray. *I suppose redemption is possible, for this one,* she'd thought with little sympathy; I've already witnessed a few miracles, this night.

Between them, Lisabetta and Julian then stuffed the dead man into his own barrel, and had waded in the river so as to float it toward the deeper water, where they watched it sink from sight.

"You should hide away in the Abbey for a time," he'd cautioned in a low voice. "Georges will put it about that you have left for Rome. In the meantime, we will advise the Empress."

She'd nodded, thoroughly unsettled by this sequence of events and trying to decide which was the more unsettling—that Rochon would dare to murder her, or that Julian had given her a glimpse of his true feelings.

And so—as a result of her brush with death—Rochon had been hauled before Napoleon himself, and forced to disclaim that he had any connection to the plot whilst Lisabetta had been given the sweet, sweet, knowledge that the man she'd adored all her life felt the same way about her.

The daunting fact remained, however, that he was a priest—and not the sort of priest who was all for show, like Tallyrand, but the sort of priest who would never, ever betray his holy vows. And so, she'd continued on with her travels and her assignments, wondering if she'd ever meet a man who could supplant her affection for her very first love, and knowing that it would be best if she stayed away from him, now that she knew she was a temptation. She may not have been an honorable woman—far from it; but he was an honorable man, and she'd little choice but to respect that. In a way, it was half the reason she loved him.

And so, things had continued in this vein until that rather wonderful night, just a month ago, when —ironically—Eugenie had taken a turn for the worse and Lisabetta had been hurriedly summoned, since it seemed her sister would not survive much longer.

Lisabetta had paced in the woman's quarters, heartsick and watching out the window at the candle that burned all night in the infirmary's antechamber. An ordinary physician could not be called-in for fear their deception would be revealed, but she knew that Julian was the equal of any physician, and that he would use all of his formidable knowledge to try to save her sister.

And—miracle of miracles—Eugenie had indeed survived the night, to the gratitude of an exhausted Lisabetta, who was then smuggled into her sister's bedside to clasp her limp hand tightly, and try to assure her that the worst was behind them.

"No—I am not afraid of death," Eugenie had whispered, her eyes hollow and over-bright. "I know you and Angelique will be cared for. I am content with my life, and I have made my peace with God." Reminded, she turned her head on the pillow toward her sister, even though the effort cost her. "Did you know? Dom Julian is not a priest."

Lisabetta had stared at her in silence for a moment until she managed to find her voice. "Why do you think this, dearest?"

"I asked to make a final Confession, and he told me he was not a priest. The Hospitaller is, and so he was called in, instead."

And from that moment forward, everything had changed. Lisabetta had a very good idea as to why Dom Julian had never taken Holy Orders, even though everyone assumed that he had, and she also had a very good idea as to why the proctor had been commissioned to accompany Lisabetta when she was on the Abbey's premises. Suddenly, a bright new future beckoned; she could finally bring her life of hopeless longing to an end, so long as she could find some way to make the stubborn man fall-in with her plans—no small feat, with another war about to break out, and his precious Order on the precipice of extinction.

But she had no fears that she would eventually succeed. It was fortunate, in a way, that she'd had lived the life that she'd lived; she'd learned how to weave a scheme from the very best scheme-weavers in all the world.

CHAPTER 10

The following afternoon, Lisabetta contrived to visit Hahn in the infirmary again, being careful to make it appear as though it was merely a routine visit, and the last of her daily chores.

"*Mon Dieu*," she hissed to the Indiaman in all annoyance. "What are you about?"

She'd gone to visit him under the guise of writing another letter, but she'd started chiding him in a low voice the moment she put pen to paper. It had come to her attention that Dom Julian himself had visited the patient the day before, and that the two men had engaged in an animated discussion for over an hour, on unknown topics.

Unrepentant, the patient shrugged. "It is not my fault; the Director asked if I was familiar with the new discoveries for treatment of the falling sickness."

"Don't be distracted, and don't be beguiled." Lisabetta scolded. "He is a shrewd operator, beneath his mild exterior."

"I am not beguiled," Hahn protested. "We are both interested in the new medical discoveries."

"*Mon Dieu*," she repeated in all exasperation. "Save me from foolish men."

"I gave nothing away," Hahn defended himself.

"So, you may think. Do not indulge him further."

"I do not take orders from you," he pointed out, stung.

There was a small pause, and then she softened her tone. "You are new to the game," she explained, "and it shows. You will swiftly see there is not a hair's breadth of difference betwixt all of them—all of these men, who send you forth to risk yourself. A few may be sorrier than the others that you are dead, but only for a minute, before they go on to move the next chess piece. Trust no one."

He regarded her for a moment. "And why should I trust you?"

"You should trust me least of all," she advised.

"It is all very confusing," he admitted in a meek tone that didn't fool her for a moment.

"You have only to pay attention to your one task; the masquerade ball is at week's end, and it is very important that you do not move from your post."

"Understood," he replied, and then added in a circumspect tone, "I understand there is a jewel to be handed over."

"You understand correctly. An emerald, as a show of good faith."

He raised his brows. "And it is—"

"As though I would give it to you," she breathed in exasperation. "*Peste*, but you have much to earn."

He shrugged. "I only wonder if this treasure exists. Many have known of it, and men are greedy; I am surprised it still exists."

She arched a brow in surprise. "Your master says this?"

"No; my master keeps his own counsel."

"As should you," she scolded. "You have told me too much already—you must not assume anyone is a friend or a foe, if you wish to survive. And do not be distracted; instead listen carefully to everything you hear—you never know when a bit of information will be useful, later on. Above all, do not be distracted by kindly Directors who show a flattering interest."

With a gleam, he replied, "I have been warned that you may also show a flattering interest, but only until you decide to sheathe a blade into a man's back."

"Your master knows of what he speaks. Do not cross me."

"Yes, miss," he replied in a meek tone.

Exasperated, she warned, "Stay vigilant—the child will arrive soon."

"Understood," he replied, his manner suddenly grave.

CHAPTER 11

Upon emerging from the infirmary, Lisabetta's proctor informed her that Dom Julian wished to consult with her privately in his tower room. This was an ominous turn of events, since—unlike her—the Abbot tended to avoid the appearance of impropriety whenever possible. It seemed clear from the summons that he did not wish their discussion be overheard, and so she'd a good guess as to the topic he wished to discuss.

So, I am to be scolded yet again, she thought; although if every time I'm to be scolded we are left unchaperoned, it will only encourage more bad behavior on my part. It does not seem to me that the poor man has thought this through.

She entered the tower room, her features arranged in a docile expression, and saw that Julian stood near one of the windows, his posture unhappy. He looked over upon her entry, and began without preamble, "I am informed that Georges' wife died last night."

Lisabetta stared at him, the picture of abject surprise. "Sophie is *dead*? *Mon Dieu*, but I was just speaking with her yesterday."

He ignored this show of innocence, and continued implacably, "I thought we'd agreed that she would be allowed to go on as she was."

Tossing her head, Lisabetta retorted, "She was a miserable turncoat, and it was past time she was removed."

But he continued unhappy with her, and said in a stern tone, "Whilst she remained in place, Tallyrand was placated and we were able to control what he learned and what he did not. Her death will only prompt him to find another spy—perhaps one that we cannot control as easily."

Lisabetta raised an indifferent shoulder. "I have every confidence that you can out-spy Monsieur Tallyrand, *mon Abbé*."

"And I would be remiss if I did not remind you that you mustn't kill people, Lisabetta."

"You did," she reminded him.

"I'd no choice, and I've made my contrition."

"Well, I hope you didn't tell your Confessor too many details—you were half-naked, at the time."

"It is no joking matter—"

"No, indeed; *tiens*, it is half the reason I'd hoped you would marry me."

"Lisabetta," he said heavily. "Enough."

There was a small silence.

"If you *were* to marry me," she ventured, "you could attempt my redemption, and cure my murderous ways."

But his reply was unyielding. "As I have told you, I cannot marry—I am needed here. And in any event, you must marry someone powerful, like Corvairre—someone with enough authority to check the British."

"That is true," she acknowledged a bit sadly. "And it is of all things ironic; I must look to marry someone of a higher standing than you, even though I am baseborn and without my treasure, I could not even look for marriage from you in the first place."

But he remained unmoved. "You are trying to manipulate me, and I do not appreciate it."

Abandoning her pose, she admitted a bit crossly, "It is beyond annoying, that you know me so well."

"Well enough to know what you are about; you are changing the subject, and we are discussing Sophie's murder."

She wheedled, "Murder is such a harsh word—"

"You will tell me what your gambit is, Lisabetta," he interrupted. "And sooner rather than later."

"Sophie had to be eliminated," she informed him bluntly. "And I cannot tell you why."

There was a long pause whilst he stared at her, his brows drawn together. "I do not appreciate being made to play blind man's bluff."

"I know, and I am sorry for it," she replied sincerely. "I wish I was free to say more." Carefully, she added, "I do not think you would disapprove of my ends, however much you disapprove of my means."

But he was not willing to entertain this excuse, and advised, "The ends can never justify the means, if the means is murder."

"Then it looks as though I will never be justified," she retorted.

In the ensuing silence, he bowed his head and offered in a more conciliatory tone, "Forgive me, I am over-harsh."

A bit ashamed that she'd snapped at him, she replied, "And you must forgive me, in turn; I promise that I am not trying to drive you mad."

Meeting her eyes again, he asked, "Tell me the truth; was it the Englishman who sought Sophie's death?"

She shook her head. "No, I am not working for the Englishman. Instead, the Englishman is working for me."

Unable to hide his surprise, he stared at her. "What does this mean? Surely you don't intend to marry him?"

"No—I must marry someone who can *counter* the English," she reminded him patiently

"Then what you say makes little sense."

She blew out a breath. "I know, but I cannot say more. I am sorry, Julian."

Thoroughly frustrated, he frowned at her. "Surely, you cannot mean to draw Tallyrand's attention?"

There was a small silence, as Lisabetta thought a bit crossly that it was of all things annoying this man was so clever—although to be fair, that was a large part of the reason she loved him so much; he was one of the very few who could out-think her. "Fah, Julian—you forget that I am Monsieur Tallyrand's faithful servant."

He cast her an ironic look—none knew better that he that her allegiances were flexible—and persisted, "I cannot understand your actions, Lisabetta—surely you would not have Tallyrand take a more pointed interest; he may decide to remove Angelique."

This was—unfortunately—a very real problem; Tallyrand had fathered more than a few illegitimate children, and such was his power that he acknowledged them openly, knowing none would dare criticize. Eugenie had been foolish enough to engage in a brief *affaire* with the notorious minister—arising from an assignment that had become a bit too tangled—and when she'd fallen pregnant, Dom Julian had moved quickly to secret the child—and Eugenie—so that the two could remain under his protection, with Tallyrand raising no objection at the time, since Josephine wouldn't be best pleased to hear about his affair with one of her wards.

But now, with Napoleon in exile and Josephine dead, the minister could easily decide that he wanted to add Angelique to his own household, and in the course of time, barter her into an alliance that was beneficial to him. It was an outcome that must be avoided at all costs; as Lisabetta well-knew, a man's illegitimate daughter could serve as a convenient pawn in his quest for power, and she was determined that Angelique would never be used as such.

But to Julian, Lisabetta only said in a placating tone, "You worry overmuch, I think; even as we speak, Monsieur Tallyrand is beating-out fires in Vienna, and trying to save his own skin—his and the King's. The man cannot be bothered with us, and Angelique is but one of many, after all. A shocking state of affairs for a clergyman, but there you are."

"Nevertheless, Sophie's death puts Angelique at risk," he reiterated. "And Tallyrand needn't step as carefully, now that the Emperor is no longer curbing his ways."

This, in reference to the fact that when he was in power, Napoleon had demanded that Tallyrand marry his long-time mistress—although it did not do much to help the man's reputation. Tallyrand's mistress had left her own husband for him, and thus her subsequent marriage to Tallyrand was seen as invalid in the eyes of the Church.

"I am not so foolish as to invite Tallyrand's interest," she soothed. "I promise you, Angelique is but a minor concern for him."

"But the Abbey is not."

She was silent, because this was another valid point; whilst it was true that Tallyrand had arranged the deal that had allowed the Knights to maintain the Abbey, it was also becoming more and more likely that Napoleon would attempt to rise to power again. If Tallyrand decided he'd best curry favor with his former liege, he could very well reveal their charade, and the Knights would lose the Abbey on top of everything else they'd lost.

"Please don't worry, Julian," she repeated. "I promise I do not compromise Angelique, or the Abbey—I swear to it."

But—as could be expected—he wasn't placated by her perplexing refusal to tell him the whole, and he slowly shook his head in confusion. "What is your gambit, Lisabetta? I confess that I am baffled."

With a small smile, she replied, "I am seeing to your future, *Monsieur le Abbé*, since you are so kindly seeing to mine."

CHAPTER 12

It was the night of the masquerade ball at the Palais Rohan, and Lisabetta stood in one of the retiring rooms that flanked the main ballroom, watching the activity through a slit in the heavy curtains that were draped across the room's entry. She was dressed in all her finery and dripping in jewels—as was appropriate for her purposes—and held her gold-laced mask in one careless hand. The participants would be all masked, mainly so that they could deny being present if it ever became needful to do so.

These balls were held on occasion, in this neutral-friendly region of France, so that frank conversations could be held amongst persons who would not be able to hold such conversations under normal circumstances. It was always the way of things; those who held high positions tended to sort things out for themselves, regardless of what the general populace was told.

There; she recognized Antoine the fishmonger as one of the early arrivals—now wearing a domino and mask, and adopting the general appearance of a wealthy gentleman. It was a good sign that he'd shown up so promptly; Tallyrand's camp would presume that Darton was the one who'd killed Sophie—since the missing operative had been spotted by Lisabetta in the area—and such a turn of events would only increase the level of anxiety within certain breasts. Few knew that Sophie spied for Tallyrand—not to mention that few knew of Angelique's true parentage. It would thus be presumed that Darton was aware of one of Tallyrand's best-kept secrets, with the additional presumption that the woman's death was part of some plot against him.

Lisabetta could feel Dom Julian step-up quietly behind her, even though he'd said nothing. It was always this way—as though she'd a special sense that alerted her, whenever he was nearby.

"I am told the Count Vassily has arrived from St. Petersburg," he offered, behind her.

"Has he? I've not spotted him." She glanced at him over her shoulder, taking in his changed appearance. He was dressed in a black domino and mask, and playing the role of minor nobility—which indeed he was, although few knew of it.

"You look very dashing," she observed, turning to peer through the slit in the curtain once again. "You must avoid the Countess Ormandie, though; she is on the hunt for a new lover."

"She looks for a wealthy Englishman, as she has run out of money and must leave the Continent."

"You know *everything*," she said, in all admiration.

"I wish that were the case," he replied in a mild tone.

She decided to make no reply, and continued with her scrutiny of the ballroom, making note of who stood where, and who spoke to whom. Julian's people might be able to ferret-out facts, but there was no substitute for observing how others interacted and drawing one's own conclusions. Indeed, this particular talent had served her very well, over the years.

He remarked, "The Baron Covairre should be arriving soon."

She sighed. "Ah, yes—my worthy suitor. I would almost hope for Monsieur Rochon to show up, and challenge him for my hand. It would make for a far more interesting evening—although I imagine Rochon does not dance well."

"I think it unlikely that Monsieur Rochon will attend, although I imagine he regrets it very much."

Hearing the nuance to his tone, she glanced quickly back at him again. "Oh? What have you heard?"

With a trace of satisfaction, he reported, "I have heard that the gentleman has been unavoidably detained in Spain."

At this astonishing news, she turned around to

stare at him. "No," she breathed. *"Sainte Mère de Dieu*, who has managed such a thing?"

"The Spanish guerrillas, I am told. They bore a grudge."

"*El Halcon*," she guessed. "Remind me never to cross him."

"Indeed," he agreed.

With renewed concentration, she went back to her scrutiny, taking careful note of who was speaking with whom, and who was ignoring whom.

"You wear the Apostle necklace? Do you think it wise?"

He referred to the medieval necklace she wore around her neck; an ornate circlet of gold filigree with precious gems set along its length—12 different gemstones, each one carved with the likeness of the Apostle that the gem represented. Absently, she drew her fingers along it. "I cannot hope to negotiate a marriage unless I make it clear that I have access to the St. Alban's treasure."

"Perhaps something less valuable would serve," he suggested.

She made a wry mouth. "There are different measures of value, *mon Abbé*. I won't risk my pearls, because they were given me by a King, and they will make a fine tale to tell my children."

He was silent for a moment, and then said, "I should go—I must speak with Fouçon before he meets with the French Ambassador."

He didn't like that reference to my children, she thought, and congratulated herself for planting an unwelcome image in his head. "*Bien sûr;* before you go, if you would help me with my domino, please."

She could sense his brief moment of hesitation, before he took up the satin cloak and moved closer to drape it over her shoulders. The gown she wore was cut low, and displayed her impressive décolletage to advantage—especially to someone of his height.

With some satisfaction, she thought; and so, I have given the good Abbot some things to think about—or at least two things. Tying the domino's strings at her throat, she said, "*Merci*. Wish me luck."

"There is no need," he replied a bit gravely. "You have always made your own luck."

She smiled in acknowledgment, and then drew the curtain aside to enter the ballroom; languidly surveying the crowd and plying her silk fan in a desultory fashion.

CHAPTER 13

With gratifying promptness, Lisabetta's hand was immediately claimed by a familiar face—the tall and handsome Count Vassily, who was a member of the Knights of Malta from the St. Petersburg Order. She'd the shrewd conviction that the Count was Julian's first choice for her husband, even as he pretended to favor Corvairre, the French King's candidate. After all, if she married Vassily, the treasure would remain in the Order's hands with the added benefit that she would spend the next war in St. Petersburg, and well-away from any danger; Napoleon was unlikely to venture into Russia again.

And—since Julian knew very well that she wouldn't welcome such a machination from him—instead he would play upon her rebellious nature, and subtly present the dashing Count as a more appealing alternative to the staid Corvairre. All in all, it made for an amusing diversion; Julian might think he knew her well, but she knew him well, in turn.

"Vlad," she said to the Russian man, as he swept her into a waltz. "How good to see you again."

"Where is Julian? I have much to report."

"He'll be along—he is warning Fouçon, somewhere. Have a care about how freely you speak, though; I am told that the Englishman will be here, and he has ears everywhere."

The Count smiled his charming smile. "Better that I have a care because you are here and laden with jewels—you make a tempting picture, Lisabetta."

"I am laden with bait because I am looking for a husband—and the sooner the better, with the Empress dead." She paused, as they swayed along the dance floor, and then added, "I understand she fell ill when your Tsar came to visit."

He grimaced slightly. "Unfortunate timing, is all. Although it is never a good idea to delve too deeply into such occurrences. Your necklace is exquisite."

"Don't be tempted to lift it," she teased. "I need it for my dowry."

"This is so? Then I am half-inclined to marry you myself."

"*Hélas*, our marriage would not further my aims, as much as I am tempted." She was being diplomatic; in truth, she found him completely ineligible, being as he was approximately her own age and would be hard-pressed to out-think her.

Her handsome partner bent his head closer to

hers. "Come now; you would enjoy the Tsar's court—it makes Napoleon's look paltry."

"I do not look to marry into your Order, you are all so tediously honorable."

He laughed aloud, and spun her rather faster than he should. "I am tempted to show you otherwise."

With a smile to show there were no hard feelings, she added, "And if you would, tell Julian that I don't appreciate this gambit."

He laughed aloud at being so easily caught-out. "I wouldn't mind marrying you, Lisabetta—I swear it, upon my soul."

"And I am grateful for the compliment," she replied graciously. "But nonetheless, I don't appreciate the gambit."

"Unfair," he countered. "You are the queen of gambits."

"With good reason," she agreed mildly. "Now that you don't have to pretend to woo me, tell me all the gossip—I've been locked away in the Abbey for a month, and climbing the walls with boredom. I understand Monsieur Rochon has been detained in Spain."

"I hear the same—it is nothing short of a miracle, and I would very much like to hear the particulars. Do you know where he is being held?"

She shook her head with regret. "I do not—I've only just heard the rumor. What is the news from St. Petersburg? I hear the Tsar is seeking the whole of Prussia, and that the Congress is very unhappy about it."

"The Tsar looks to acquire Prussia," he agreed. "Although it is hard to know which rumors to believe; at present, his court is an ocean of intrigue—even worse than the Congress."

"Is it? Then I may reconsider your offer," she teased. "I would happily swim in an ocean of intrigue."

He laughed again, his eyes alight as they continued their whirling dance. "Here is some gossip you will appreciate; the Count Khilkov has returned to St. Petersburg with his new bride, and he dares anyone to whisper a word against her." He gave Lisabetta a significant look.

"Oh, yes; she is another stray-relation, like me—*tiens*, we are practically related, this bride of his. I can only wish her well."

Fairly, the gentleman offered, "He seems very fond of her, despite her heritage."

"Or because of it," Lisabetta offered dryly

"Or because of it," he agreed with a chuckle. "Eugenie will be disappointed that he is so fond—she sought Khilkov's bed, I think."

Lisabetta's brow immediately grew stormy. "Eugenie seeks everyone's bed, and the less I hear of her, the better."

"Your pardon," he offered, contrite. "Do you know what has happened to her? No one has heard; it is as though she has disappeared from the face of the earth."

"I know not, nor do I care," Lisabetta replied in a tart tone.

He persisted, "Julian has said nothing of her?"

With a raised brow, she teased, "Oh-ho; do you think Julian has fallen victim to my wicked sister? He wouldn't be the first holy man who has."

With a gleam, her companion chuckled at this absurdity. "Unlikely—the mind boggles."

"It would explain why no one has seen her—he's locked her away for himself."

He chuckled again, and as the strains of the waltz came to an end, he asked, "Shall we have a walk in the town, tomorrow? I would hear of your adventures—the *affaire* de Gilles, and that unfortunate contretemps in Flanders."

"*Certainment*, but nowhere so crowded; come to Beaulieu, instead, and we will go rowing on the river. Then I can tell my tales freely."

"Very good. Shall I call at the Abbey?"

"Better to meet at the docks," she cautioned. "I don't want Julian to think that his gambit has borne fruit."

He laughed yet again. "I may yet change your mind," he teased. "What time?"

"Early—before my proctor rises," she decided. "Or, we can meet in the evening, if morning would be too much of a hardship for you."

"You wound me; I rise early."

"Very well, then."

With a smile, he then relinquished her to her next dance partner—shooting her one last gleam of amusement as he walked away, since her new partner was none other than the grey-eyed

Englishman.

CHAPTER 14

"Lisabetta," the English spymaster greeted her, as he led her into position. "You look lovely."

"My necklace certainly does."

"Along with the bosom it rests upon."

"My best asset," she acknowledged fondly. "I must use whatever weapons I can."

With a small smile, he placed his hand at her waist, and took up her hand for the next waltz. "How goes the war?"

Thoughtfully, she replied, "There has been some progress, I believe."

"Has there? None that I have noticed."

"You don't know him as well as I do, *mon ami*. And have a care; he's penetrated your Indiaman already."

The grey-eyed man's expression did not change, but she knew he was annoyed. "You are certain?"

"Julian is very shrewd, monsieur—and very good at keeping his own counsel. Do not be deceived."

"Yet he allows the man to remain in place?"

"I think our Abbot wishes to extract what information he can from him, whilst the man remains unaware that he's been penetrated."

"Ah. I don't have high hopes, then."

"Your Indiaman is a bit rash," she agreed. "And far too impudent."

With a nod of acknowledgement, her companion admitted, "Yes, he is new. Perhaps after more seasoning, he could become more adept."

"If he survives that long."

"If he survives that long," the Englishman agreed. "We shall see."

They navigated the floor for a few more turns, whilst Lisabetta reflected that—whilst the spymaster was a competent dancer, he had none of Vassily's *panache*. Hard on this thought, her partner asked, "Tell me what the Count Vassily said to you."

She laughed as though he'd said something witty. "And why would I do that?"

"Because Castlereagh is concerned that the Tsar of Russia is going to insist on the annexation of Prussia. Vassily has the Tsar's ear, and may know his intent."

Castlereagh was the British representative at the Congress in Vienna, and so Lisabetta responded with a derisive sound. "And the British are horrified to think that anyone should try to amass power, other than themselves."

"As cynical as you are beautiful," the spymaster pronounced. "I should marry you, in truth."

"The Count is of a like mind; he has suggested that I might enjoy the Tsar's court."

He raised his brows with interest. "Oh? Has Russia entered into the marriage-stakes?"

"So, it appears."

He considered this for a moment, his manner unruffled as they danced a few more steps. "Perhaps you would be kind enough to see what you can learn from him about the Tsar's intentions. I will make it worth your while."

She smiled up at him vivaciously, hoping that Julian was watching. "I can make no guarantees."

With a return smile that didn't quite reach his eyes, he emphasized, "I will pay handsomely for any information you might obtain."

She threw back her head and laughed, as though she were enjoying herself immensely. "We can keep handing the same bounty back and forth between us, like a child's game. I wonder who will walk off with it, at the end."

"One can hope we both walk off with what is most important to us."

Thus reminded, she took a quick survey of the dancers around them, glancing sidelong through the slits of her mask. "Has the Baron Corvairre yet arrived?"

"Not as yet—he is one who likes to make a grand entrance."

She twisted her mouth in amusement. "Be kind; I may yet have to marry him, if the King has his way."

"I would lay odds on you against the French King, Lisabetta. I cannot foresee even fat Louis bringing you to heel."

"Speaking of which, I would take this opportunity to bait my trap, if you don't mind."

"Of course; where shall I leave you?"

"The northwest corner," she directed, as the strains of the waltz reached their crescendo.

"Very well," he said, and steered them over to the area she'd indicated. "May I call upon you tomorrow morning? I should keep up the pressure."

"In the afternoon instead, *s'il vous plait;* I will have a busy morning."

As the dance concluded, he bowed over her hand in a lingering fashion for the benefit of anyone who might be watching. "Until tomorrow, then."

She curtseyed low, the stiff brocade of her gown rustling as she did so. "Until tomorrow, monsieur."

CHAPTER 15

This area of the ballroom was nearest the woman's retiring room, and as a consequence it featured a small coterie of women who had gathered together to gossip and admire one another. Lisabetta joined them—it always paid to be friendly to the women, as oftentimes men were foolish enough to disclose important information to their bed-companions.

The Countess Ormandie duly complimented Lisabetta's hair and gown, and then observed archly, "The gentlemen are all like bees to a flower, *ma chère*."

Lanquidly, Lisabetta waved her fan. "Are they? I feel as though it is I who am the bee."

The Countess nodded knowingly. "Yes—there are rumors that you must marry, now that the Empress is dead."

With a snap, Lisabetta shut her fan. "*Peste*—I cannot bear to think about it, and so I won't. Tell me of your liaison with de Bournais, instead; he is smitten, I hear."

There was a tiny pause, whilst the other woman's color rose a bit. "He is rather annoying, to be frank—clings to me excessively."

"How tedious; you must cut him adrift, and find someone less *banal*," Lisabetta advised.

"Yes. If you have any suggestions, I will listen," the other replied. "Is the Count Vassily eligible? Although I would do not wish to step on your toes, *ma belle*."

This is not true, of course; the Countess would happily trample Lisabetta—or anyone else in her way—if she was set upon making a conquest. Nevertheless, Lisabetta made a sound of regret. "*Hélas* for any such plans; the Count Vassily will be leaving town shortly."

"*Peste*; this wretched Congress—it takes everyone's attention, and draws all the eligible men to Vienna. Who is that, over there with Vassily? He is new to town, I think."

Spreading her fan open again, Lisabetta casually took a glance over to where Julian was speaking in quiet tones with Count Vassily—no doubt plotting the man's courtship of herself. "He is a handsome one, isn't he? Although I will give you fair warning; he was in the Empress' retinue at Paris, and Madame Tolante believes he gave her the pox."

Making a discreet sound of disapproval, the Countess replied, "Ah—many thanks for the warning.

Do let me know if you hear of any eligible men—perhaps an Englishman; always an easy conquest, since they cannot help but see a Frenchwoman as a trophy."

"My last dance-partner was an Englishman," Lisabetta offered innocently. "A very intriguing man."

The Countess' sharp gaze skewed over the assembly and rested on the grey-eyed man, who was standing by the punch bowl with a rather bored expression. "He seems rather ordinary," she commented behind her fan. "And not much of a dancer, which does not bode well for the bedroom."

"I believe he deals in jewels," Lisabetta advised.

The other lady immediately brightened. "Does he? I may have to make his acquaintance, then."

With all goodwill, Lisabetta offered, "He will much admire your garnets—they are such a lovely color."

There was the barest pause. "Yes—I decided not to wear my diamonds, tonight," her companion replied, with an air of indifference. "Too risky."

Lisabetta swayed her fan. "You are wise; I fear I am a little foolish, to wear my finest to a gathering such as this." Hard on this pronouncement, she fingered her earlobes, and then exclaimed, "Fah—wouldn't you know it? I've lost an earring, and these are my favorites—I must go search for it."

She departed from her companion, ostensibly scrutinizing the floor, and walked a few paces until she maneuvered near to Antoine, the erstwhile fishmonger. "Sir," she addressed him coyly, fluttering her fan.

"Oh—would you care to dance, mademoiselle?" the big man asked gallantly. "I will warn you that I'm not very good at it."

"No—it is a quadrille, and I must speak with you privately. Walk with me instead, whilst I search for my earring."

As they bent to search the floor, she murmured, "I bear grave information. The Count Vassily is the Tsar's confidante, and he tells me the Tsar is very unhappy that Tallyrand secretly courts the British against him. And so, the Tsar plans to reveal your master's double-dealings, as well as his complicity in the death of the Duc d'Enghein."

Hearing this, Antoine caught his breath in acute distress.

She nodded, seeing his reaction. "It gets worse, *mon ami*; he will reveal that your master forced himself on an aristocratic woman, and that she bore a child that he has kept hidden. The Tsar knows the British will look for any excuse to expel Tallyrand from the Congress."

Thoroughly alarmed, Antoine replied, "This is indeed very serious. What did you tell the Count?"

"I thought it best to pretend indifference; I told him that I know nothing of these matters, and if the Russians seek to betray Tallyrand to the British, I will not stand in their way." She paused. "I expect to be paid for this information."

"Of course," Antoine assured her, even as she

could see that his mind was working furiously. "I must depart for Vienna immediately, but I will leave your payment in the usual place."

"Many thanks," she replied. Then—so it would not seem that she was speaking over-much with a minor player—she bade him farewell and wandered from his side. It would take approximately one week for Antoine to travel to Vienna, she calculated. And then a week to return—perhaps less, depending upon how dire Tallyrand believed the situation to be.

He thoughts were interrupted when a young man —an attaché to the Austrian Ambassador—asked her to dance, no doubt emboldened by the fact that all her partners, thus far, hadn't been high-level aristos.

"*Je suis fatigué*," she explained kindly, as she waved her fan. "Many thanks, but I think I must take some air, instead."

CHAPTER 16

Plying her fan as though she were overheated, Liisabetta stepped through one of the doors that opened onto the balcony, and then was not surprised to discover that Dom Julian soon joined her there, standing at a small distance. So that it would not appear that he'd deliberately sought her out, she raised her fan in a flirtatious manner and stepped over to address him. "I fear that you have lost your allure, *mon Abbé*; Countess Ormandie gives you a wide berth."

But he was in no mood, and observed in a level tone, "I may have lost my allure, but it seems that you have lost an earring."

She ducked her head to smooth-out a wrinkle on one of her gloves. "Yes—it is of all things annoying. I must keep searching for it."

"Perhaps you could search the Englishman's waistcoat pocket."

Feigning surprise, she protested, "I am astonished that you suggest I lay hands on the Englishman."

"In turn, I am astonished that you are willing to collaborate with him, yet again. You learned a hard lesson, once."

So; here was a very intriguing show of emotion from the good Abbot, and Lisabetta hid her extreme satisfaction. With a small sigh, she advised, "I have learned many hard lessons, *mon Abbé*; I fear you will have to be more specific."

But time was short, and so he asked bluntly, "Why do you pay him, Lisabetta? I cannot think that you would invite his scrutiny into the Abbey's affairs."

Lisabetta decided that her best defense was to go on offense, and so she tossed her head. "Fah—I am not the only one who is scheming; did you truly think the Count Vassily would be to my taste? Shame on you, Julian."

There was a small silence, and then he offered in a more conciliatory tone, "Forgive me; it seemed a sensible solution. And if you left for St. Petersburg, you would no longer be at-risk in the coming war."

With an edge to her tone, she corrected, "You mean to say that the St. Alban's treasure would no longer be at-risk."

"Acquit me of greed, Lisabetta."

There was another small silence, and then she softened her tone in turn. "I do," she admitted. "You meant well, I think."

"But do you? You have not yet answered my

question about why you pay the Englishman, as much as you hope to distract me from the topic."

"Please—let's not quarrel, Julian; I have the very best of intentions, but I am afraid you must trust me in this."

He tilted his head in an open gesture of skepticism. "Must I? I believe the India patient belongs to the Englishman, and that you are aware of this."

She sighed, and closed her eyes briefly. "He does," she admitted. "Fah, but the Englishman did not send me his best."

Amused by this answer despite himself, he bent his head closer to hers and persisted, "What is the gambit, Lisabetta? And why can't you tell me?"

"It involves another means that is justified by the ends," she replied honestly. "You would be horrified."

He frowned slightly, searching her eyes. "Then why do you plan it?"

"Because I am not at all horrified by such things," she explained. "*Tout à fait*, they are my stock-in-trade."

But he continued perplexed. "It appears to me that you risk yourself—and that you risk my Order."

"No," she corrected. "I am saving myself, and I am saving your Order."

With a knit brow, he contemplated her silently for a moment. "Are you? I wonder—" he said slowly, "I wonder if you are trying to force my hand."

Exasperated, she retorted, "If I must acquit you of

greed, you must surely acquit me of trying to force you to do something you'd rather not do. I am ashamed of you for thinking it, Julian."

"Yes," he replied. "I beg your pardon."

"Good," she said briskly. "Now that it's settled, please don't pack-off the Indiaman down the river; I need him posted at the Abbey."

"Nothing is as yet settled," he pointed out in a firm tone. "And I will know his aim, please—I will not have an instigator within my walls."

She debated, and then admitted, "He watches. You have shown yourself far too trusting."

He considered this for a silent moment, as the strains of the next waltz began to drift in from the ballroom. "But surely, you do not trust the Englishman over me?"

"I trust no one, save God," she replied, rather pleased that a glimpse of jealousy had reappeared. "And despite what you might think, you and He are not one and the same."

"Unfair," he protested.

"*You* are the one who is being unfair—*Sainte Mère de Dieu*, but I am working like a horse in harness."

Shaking his head slightly, he asked in all bewilderment, "Why can't you tell me your aim, in all of this?"

"But I have already explained it to you—my aim is to save everyone and everything. It is a complicated business, to bring it all about."

He met her eyes. "So complicated that it requires giving the Englishman an emerald?"

She assured him, "You mustn't worry; it was only paste."

His brows drew down in disapproval. "The Englishman is not one to be trifled with, Lisabetta."

"No. But then, neither am I, *mon Abbé*."

"Lisabetta—"

"Ah—the Baron Corvairre has arrived," she interrupted, listening to the commotion behind them. "Please don't worry, Julian; I will give you a full report in the morning."

Lifting her fan, she then turned to make an unhurried progress through the balcony doors, very much pleased because—despite the fact that it was not easy to tell, through his mask—Lisabetta was fairly certain that Julian's gaze kept straying to her décolletage.

CHAPTER 17

"My dear Baron," Lisabetta gaily greeted the older, more distinguished man. He was an attaché to the court of France's new King, and was another diplomat—rather like Tallyrand—who'd managed to navigate the past few years relatively unscathed, mainly due to his ability to predict how events were likely to unfold, and to be discreetly absent when those events might threaten his interests. He was known to be a trusted courtier, and well-respected as one of the King's representatives in the ongoing negotiations.

With old-world courtesy, he bowed. "My dear Lisabetta, you are lovely, indeed; may I have the honor of this dance?"

"You may," she agreed, and smiled up at him as he led her onto the dance floor. "I have been longing to see you, and here you are."

"And I have been longing to see the Apostle necklace," he replied with a dry little smile.

"Although the bosom they rest upon would tempt even the Apostles to sin, I think."

She laughed. "A very pretty compliment."

"Allow me to offer my hand in marriage, and you will hear many more."

They took a smooth turn around the floor, Lisabetta very much amused. "You make quick work, *monsieur le Baron*."

Gallantly, he offered, "I will confess I am as tempted as the Apostles."

"Tempted by my dowry, more like."

"You wound me," he accused with a little smile. "But such practicalities must be addressed, of course. The House of Bourbon will be happy to give you any assurances you wish—the King pretends to be confident, but he knows he sits on a precarious throne, especially with the Emperor rattling his sword again. You need safety, my King needs funding, and I am only too happy to be the liaison by which both are accomplished."

"You are very well-placed to offer protection," she agreed.

"I am, indeed. And I could ask for nothing more than to have a wife of your beauty gracing my home."

"*Des Fontaines*; I hear the gardens are lovely."

He made a polite little grimace. "Unfortunately, I have been forced to move my household to Paris, for the time being."

"Oh?" she searched her memory, trying to remember the particulars. "Did the estate belong to your dear, departed wife? Such a lovely woman—I miss her sorely."

"No—brigands torched the place; an unfortunate dispute about a Murillo painting."

Lisabetta's brow cleared. "Ah." When Napoleon had conquered Spain, his *Afrancesados* had promptly looted the cathedrals of much of their priceless artwork. It seemed, however, that this did not sit well with the Spanish guerrillas who'd fought so ferociously during the war, and so—in retaliation—there'd been a rash of counter-robberies, coupled with arson fires.

"Yes—deplorable, that such lawlessness can flourish."

Diplomatically, Lisabetta did not point out that the artwork was stolen to begin with, and instead declared, "It is an amazement to me that there are any honorable men left in this world. Save you, of course—so honorable you are willing to propose marriage to a less than honorable woman."

"I would not have it any other way, Lisabetta; I leap at the chance."

She smiled, rather pleased by his flattery even as she knew it was practiced and insincere. "You have reason to be so generous, I think. I may be a stray-relation, but I was very fortunate in who those relations were."

He laughed, not at all discomfited by her plain-speaking. "Precisely. And at the risk of being *très gauche*, I would imagine the King would like us to come to terms as quickly as possible."

She sighed. "Yes. This poor treasure; it gets handed here and handed there and handed back again—a shame, that something of such value has become naught more than a bargaining-chip."

Fairly, he pointed out, "I imagine it has been used as such from the moment it was amassed, mademoiselle, and by far more desperate people."

"Yes. I suppose I should thank *le bon Dieu* that Josephine loved jewelry, and that she was so fond of my mother—and my mother of her."

"Such are the caprices of life. All in all, it has worked out very well."

With a smile, she agreed, "It did, indeed; they both survived—and against all odds."

"More than survived; each flourished," he declared. "Two clever women who fashioned their own fates, in these turbulent times. Rather like yourself, mademoiselle."

She laughed. "Again, a very pretty compliment, but believe me, *monsieur le Baron*, it would have been far easier if fate had done the fashioning."

"If you say. And here I stand, ready to fashion your fate as you would wish. May I call upon you tomorrow?"

"No need; I will marry you, I suppose—I truly don't have much choice in the matter."

"You have made me the happiest of men," he replied with a touch of amusement. "I will have the settlements drawn-up."

"Only don't come calling tomorrow," she warned, "I will be very busy."

CHAPTER 18

D espite her promise to give Dom Julian a debriefing, the following morning saw Lisabetta at Georges' house early, ostensibly paying a condolence call to the new widower.

The knocker had been removed from the door, with a black wreath hanging in its place as Lisabetta quickly slipped inside. She then entered the kitchen to see that Georges was dressed in mourning—as was only appropriate—even though he was seated at the breakfast table and playing a raucous game of slap-deck with Angelique, the child giggling as she slapped her cards down.

"Can the neighbors hear you roaring?" Lisabetta asked with a smile. "They will suspect you do not mourn your wife overmuch."

"They will not fault me," Georges replied, as he slapped another card. "And the local widows will soon come courting, to roar along with me."

"Mam'selle Lisabetta," Angelique offered, her eyes bright as she held up her markers. "Look—I am winning."

"Indeed, you are," Lisabetta agreed, running a fond hand over the girl's head. "And I have been working like a horse in harness to make certain of it."

"Take my place," Georges offered, as he rose to his feet—rather easily, for one who was generally considered to be infirm. "You can lose to *la petite mademoiselle* for a change."

"Could we play with your dollhouse instead, *ma chère*?" Lisabetta asked the little girl. "I will come join you in a moment, after I make tea for Georges."

"Yes, mam'selle—but Mitta's hair is tangled; I tried to braid it like you do, but it did not work."

"I will remedy this problem, then; fetch a brush for Mitta, and I will come in just a moment."

As soon as the little girl left the room, Georges followed Lisabetta over to the hearth. "What is needed?" he asked in a low tone.

"You will take Angelique to the Abbey for another visit—I will send a signal when it is time," she replied, as she hung the kettle. "Make certain to smuggle her dolls in the bottom of a basket; she will not be returning."

He nodded. "And her clothes?"

Lisabetta considered. "Another dress, perhaps—but only if you can manage it, I wish no alarms to be raised. And if you can deliver her whilst Jacques is out fishing, that would be best."

Gravely, he nodded again. "I understand."

She reached into her sleeve to remove a diamond stickpin that had been secreted therein. "Here's a fine bauble; it was the Baron Corvairre's, and now it is yours."

He chuckled as he accepted the pin, turning it so that it glittered in the morning light. "I don't know as I have occasion to wear such a thing, mademoiselle."

"Then offer it to one of the widows who will come courting; someone who will be loyal to you, rather than sport a prodigious bosom."

"It is hard to look past a good bosom," he admitted.

She laughed. "I cannot argue, since this circumstance has served me well over the years."

"Sophie was a good cook," he defended, as he took the tea-caddy from its shelf. "And she was kind to Angelique; how was I do know?"

"Agreed; how is anyone to know who will turn coat? It is just as well that there will no longer be a need for Tallyrand to post a spy—it was wearisome."

He nodded, as his gaze strayed beyond the doorway, to where the little girl was arranging her dolls on the floor. "I will miss her."

Laying a fond hand on his arm, Lisabetta told him, "You have earned your peace, *mon ami*. And speaking of such, I am going rowing with a Russian gentleman this morning—we will round the point out into the river at midmorning, and stay close to the shoreline. He is far too curious about Mademoiselle Eugenie's whereabouts."

"Understood," he replied, his face brightening.

Taking their tea cups, they moved into the parlor, and as Lisabetta settled in to braid the doll's hair, Georges walked over to remove the rifle that hung over the mantle.

CHAPTER 19

A few hours later, Lisabetta returned from her rowing excursion thoroughly chilled and damp from the morning mists. With a practiced movement, she tied the rowboat to the dock's piling—taking a final, firm yank to make certain the knot was secure—and then began re-tucking her hair into its silken résille as she walked up the ramp. The mists always wreaked havoc with her hair, but fine weather may have meant witnesses, and so she could not complain.

There was one witness, however, that she hadn't anticipated; Jacques suddenly appeared at the top of the ramp, his manner openly insolent as he leaned against the railing. "*Bon jour,* mademoiselle. Did you not go out with a gentleman?"

But Lisabetta was not one to be intimidated, and replied in an even tone, "He was called away unexpectedly; a Russian gentleman, who sought whatever information I could give him about my good friend Monsieur Rochon." She then gave him a meaningful look—it seemed an opportune time to let him know she was aware of his true allegiances.

This remark seemed to have served its purpose, in that she saw a sudden trace of wariness enter the man's eyes. "Oh? And what did you tell this gentleman?"

She drew her brows down in incredulity. "Nothing. He was Russian—did you not hear me?" It went without saying that there was no love lost between Napoleon's people and the Russians.

He stood immobile, his expression unreadable—Rochon was not one who recruited fools, after all—and so she continued to tuck her hair away. "You must take heart; the rumors that Rochon was captured in Spain are only that—rumors meant to dishearten and confuse. Stay vigilant; matters are moving quickly, and I can say no more." She'd learned, long ago, that the best way to survive in this business was to take whatever threads of information one could, and then bluff as boldly as one dared.

There was a small silence, and he bent his head slightly. "Your pardon, mademoiselle—Monsieur Antoine believes you serve Monsieur Tallyrand."

Making a derisive sound, she met his eye with some amusement. "And Monsieur Antoine believes Tallyrand still serves the Emperor. He is a few steps behind, I think."

But Jacques was not one to give anything away—indeed, his unreadable gaze was rather disconcerting, but she was too practiced to let him see that he made her uneasy. Brusquely, she advised, "Antoine said that you would have my money."

But the man only shrugged, and raised his palms. "Money is in short supply. I will see what I can do."

She regarded him for an amused moment as though she admired his brashness, and then offered-up a beguiling smile, her gaze traveling along the length of his masculine form. "Perhaps we could come to terms, then; I have need of the money immediately, and I am willing to earn my pay."

Nothing loath, Jacques quickly straightened up and took a glance around. "Come, then; my wife is at my house, but we can—"

But before he could complete the sentence, she'd stepped up to his side, wresting two of his fingers back while at the same time pressing a slim blade against the artery in his throat—forcing him to stand motionless, lest he step into the blade.

Into his ear, Lisabetta hissed, "You cheat me, *bâtard.*"

Standing perfectly still, man disclaimed, "No—I do not cheat you, mademoiselle—my promise. I was only joking—"

She pressed the tip of the blade so that he drew-in a quick breath. "Where is my money?"

"It is in the stall—I swear."

For emphasis, she pressed again, slightly. "Antoine would be unhappy to hear that you are a cheat. So would your wife."

"I was only joking—I swear it, mademoiselle."

She withdrew her blade, and stepped away to slip it within her sleeve once again. "I will say no more of this, then. It is a good lesson for you—you must not be so easily distracted when a woman offers bedsport."

Rather ironically, he bowed his head as he rubbed his throat. "I will bear this in mind."

She followed him to the fishmonger's stall, watching him carefully as they walked along the dock. Hopefully her gambit had worked, and he was no longer a threat—although he was a hard one to read. With any luck, he'd think she was a fellow-operative for Rochon, and thus he wouldn't be overly-concerned about her actions over the next few days—in a way, this encounter had been a stroke of good fortune, despite its ominous nature. Antoine may be something of a genial buffoon, but Jacques was another matter entirely; Lisabetta had long experience in assessing men, and this one warranted a very cautious approach.

After retrieving the small purse of coins from the lockbox under the stall, Jacques handed it over without comment. Lisabetta paused to extract a coin, and hand it back to him. "For your wife—buy her something pretty," she advised with an ironic smile.

With a bow of his head, the man accepted the coin. "*Merci*, mademoiselle."

Lisabetta then turned to exit the market area; it never hurt to sow a bit of goodwill when one had the chance—you never knew when it might pay off, and she had the uneasy feeling that she hadn't necessarily won that encounter. It took all her discipline not to glance back at him warily, as she felt the fisherman's gaze on her retreating back.

CHAPTER 20

*H*aving much on her mind, Lisabetta trudged up the road toward the Abbey, thinking about what she should report to Julian, and wondering how soon it would be before he realized that a prominent member of his Order had disappeared whilst in her company. She was analyzing her options when she was diverted by a familiar voice.

"May I offer a ride up the hill?"

Lisabetta looked up to see Julian, pulling up in the Abbey's donkey cart and very unhappy with her, judging from the set of his jaw. With a mental sigh, she scrambled up onto the perch beside him; ah, well—she was slated to have this conversation sooner or later, so best turn it to her advantage as best she could.

Once she settled on the wooden seat and straightened out her skirts, he flicked the reins so that the donkey began pulling against the harness again.

They rode for a few moments in silence, with the only sound being the creaking of the wheels as Lisabetta decided—rather defensively—that she should be just as cross with him as he was with her. *Peste*, but it seemed that one couldn't steal a sou from the offering-plate without the Abbot of Beaulieu becoming aware of it, which meant—unfortunately—there was every possibility that he could indeed outspy the Englishman.

He broke the silence to ask in a pointed tone. "What has happened to the Count Vassily?"

He knew very well what had happened to the Count, of course, since it was the reason he'd appeared on the road beside her. Bluntly, she advised, "He was a liability, Julian. Your proffered husband inquired after Eugenie, and sought her whereabouts. There would be no good reason for him to do so."

This revelation was met with a moment's surprised silence. "Are you certain he was not making a polite inquiry?"

"I am. He also sought to discover where Rochon was being held."

There was a small pause, and then—rather heavily—he offered, "Believe me when I tell you I was not aware."

She blew out a breath. "You can't be blamed; he was a fellow Knight, and so you accepted him at face value. But not all of them are as honorable as you are, Julian; it was no surprise to me that he was compromised, considering he is a fixture at the Tsar's court." She paused, and then continued, "It may be safest to assume that other Knights in St. Petersburg are likewise compromised."

But he only replied in a grave tone, "I don't know as I would characterize anyone as 'compromised,' as much as they are reluctantly practical. My Order must curry favor with the Tsar, else it will be left with no base at all from which to do our work. I suspect the Count felt he had little choice."

Unable to resist, she cast him a glance. "So; you are saying that the ends justify the means."

But he was not going to travel down this path, and instead said firmly, "Murder is a grave sin, Lisabetta. I know you protect your sister, but you should have informed me—I protect her, also. I would have handled this problem short of killing him."

But stubbornly, she insisted, "No—I didn't want any trace of your involvement in this; the Tsar has eyes and ears everywhere, too. It seemed the best course to protect you, your Order, and Eugenie—all of you. Everyone will suspect that Napoleon's people are behind the Count's disappearance, anyway—they are gathering-up their power, again, and the Emperor holds a mighty grudge against the Tsar. We are fortunate that Jacques is close-at-hand, and would make a likely scapegoat if anyone starts making inquiries."

He was silent for a moment, as the donkey's hooves clip-clopped. "Did the Englishman aid you, in this?"

"No."

But he was openly skeptical, and glanced over at her. "It is mere coincidence, that one of his rivals has been eliminated?"

She quirked her mouth. "His only rival is Corvairre, Julian; he does not know of your gambit with Vassily—you must try to keep my suitors straight. And in any event, the Englishman will not approve of the Count's elimination, since he was hoping I could extract information from him."

Contemplating this in silence for a moment, he nodded. "I see."

"I work alone," she added lightly, thinking to obscure Georges' role.

But her companion only countered, "I believe we have already established that you are working a gambit with the Englishman—or, more properly, he is working with you."

Thus reminded that the Abbot was not so easily misled, she tried to decide how much to tell him. She couldn't give the game away; or at least, not yet—too much was at stake. But she couldn't blame him for being alarmed at how events were unfolding—after all, the quiet little village had seen two deaths in two days.

Carefully, she explained, "Yes, the Englishman is allied with me—but only so that he may achieve his own goals." She paused. "It is the nature of our business—alliances are formed and broken, depending on what is needed at the moment. It may be difficult for you to understand—you work in an honorable world, and I do not."

He thought about this for a moment, and then admitted, "I think I am most concerned because it seems that you do not trust me."

With all sincerity, she turned to him. "I do trust you, Julian—but in turn, you must trust me. I cannot tell you more—at least, not yet—but I *promise* you would approve of the goals I seek."

"If you say; but I will in turn have your promise that such a thing will not be repeated, Lisabetta."

"I hope it will not be necessary," she hedged. "And on that subject, I may as well confess that I also tussled with Jacques, this fine morning."

Alarmed, he asked, "Jacques is dead?"

"No—I wouldn't dare; the Tsar's wrath is one thing, but Rochon's is wholly another, as you and I are both aware."

"Rochon has been caged," he reminded her, with a satisfied flick of the reins.

She sighed. "It is rather sweet, that you are so naïve, *mon Abbé*."

"What happened with Jacques?"

"He decided to try to wrestle me into bed."

"*What*?" His brows drew down. "He laid hands upon you?"

Yet again, she welcomed this promising show of jealousy, and congratulated herself for planting the image in his head of a maiden in peril—a shame, that her hair was all bound-up like a nun's. "He tried, but

I made mention of his wife, which seemed to compel second thoughts."

But her companion's brow continued stormy. "Outrageous, that he would dare."

"He is not a nice man," she noted, in a massive understatement.

Julian was silent for a few moments, and then he reasoned, "You may have valid idea, though; we could launch an inquiry into the Count's death, with Jacques as a likely scapegoat. His role as Rochon's man would be exposed, and we would be rid of him."

"I am not certain that is the best idea," she replied in a doubtful tone. "Those who are his masters would know they made no such orders, and they would immediately come after anyone who'd made such a claim."

"True," he agreed with some reluctance. "Perhaps it would be best to leave the matter alone."

"Yes—I think so." She looked over at the trees for a moment, knowing that the Abbot of Beaulieu would have reasoned this out for himself, which in turn gave her the strong suspicion that she was being manipulated—which was annoying, as she was trying her best to be the one who was doing the manipulating, here.

He glanced over at her. "What did the Baron Corvairre say to you last night?"

"Nothing of importance," she replied, glossing over the small matter of his marriage proposal, and her acceptance. "Although I cannot blame you for being uneasy about him—the French King relies on England to keep his throne, and if Corvairre marries my treasure, there is every chance the King will turn it straight over to England. Which was the very reason you threw the Count Vassily my way; at least if the treasure landed with Russia, it would presumably help shore-up your Order."

"Forgive me, Lisabetta. It was ill-advised, but I promise you it was well-intentioned."

But she only smiled, as she contemplated the donkey's ears—twitching back and forth as they spoke. "*De rien*. It is not a surprise that you sought to keep what remains of the St. Alban's treasure out of England's Protestant hands."

He grimaced, slightly. "Acquit me of such a prejudice, please."

This seemed a prime opportunity to bring up a delicate subject, and so she ventured, "Yes—you seem to have no objection to the Protestants in Gottingen; you are happy to exchange scientific theories with them."

There was a small silence. Gottingen was a small city in the Prussian region of Hanover, and had long been a center for scientific research. Lisabetta had recently become aware that the good Abbot was corresponding with some of the leading purveyors of the cell theory there—discreetly, of course, since he couldn't pursue such a correspondence openly.

With a wondering shake of his head, her companion kept his gaze on the road ahead. "And how do you know of this?"

"Oh—I keep abreast of your doings, *mon Abbé*. And I would point out that the Protestants in Gottingen are much more invested in your cell theory than the Church you serve."

This, in fact, was in keeping with something she'd observed in her travels; the true scientists—much like the true clergy—had little interest in the squabbling that went on between heads of state; their focus was instead on greater, more profound things.

But—as could be expected—her companion chose to defend the Church he'd served all his life. "The cell theory is a revolutionary idea, and revolutionary ideas tend to be regarded warily until they've had time to show their value. But I do believe it is only a matter of time before the theory becomes generally accepted—especially now that it is possible to observe it with our own eyes."

"Good; then you will not have to turn coat, and become a Protestant. I was bracing myself."

He smiled, just as she'd intended. "No. But even the Church leaders can see that the world is changing, and changing rapidly."

Almost gently, she offered, "And you are longing to be part of it—part of these new discoveries."

He was silent for a moment, as the determined donkey continued with its clipping steps up the hill. "After the next war, perhaps."

But she only made an impatient sound. "There is always a 'next war', Julian; and if you and I know nothing else, we know that life is uncertain—and sometimes shorter than we'd like. You have done a fine job of trying to stay the course here at the Abbey, but I think you know that your true calling is in Gottingen."

"I must go where my Order directs, Lisabetta."

"Then ask your Order if you may go to Gottingen; no better way to serve the poor, one would think, than to cure their ills."

He did not immediately respond, but after a moment he smiled slightly, as though amused. Seeing this, she asked, "What? What is it?"

"This is your own version of the Count Vassily."

She stared at him for a moment, much struck, and then had to chuckle. "Yes; I suppose it is—an attempt to meddle, and arrange the future for you. My idea is better than yours, though—promise me you will consider it."

"We can't always arrange matters to suit ourselves—as much as we like to believe we can." He paused, and his attitude grew a bit grave. "And on that subject, I must tell you that Sebastian seems to have taken a turn for the worse, this morning. I am afraid his time grows short."

"No," Lisabetta breathed, staring at him in acute dismay.

With all sympathy, he offered, "There is little left that can be done; indeed, it is surprising that he did not succumb months ago."

Suddenly sober, she turned to regard the road ahead. "I need to visit him—today."

He pulled at the reins as they came to a halt

before the Abbey's entry. "Do you think it wise? The Indiaman remains in the infirmary."

"I must see him," she repeated. "It is very important, Julian."

Reading her expression, he nodded. "Of course. I am so sorry, Lisabetta."

"You don't know the half of it," she replied softly.

CHAPTER 21

❦

And so, as soon as she was able, Lisabetta visited the infirmary—ostensibly to deliver mail to the patients, and chafing that she had to present an unhurried façade, even though she was desperate to assess her sister's condition for herself.

"I've a letter for you," she said to Hahn, bending to speak to him briefly. "It says that a little girl will come to visit, and that you will miraculously improve."

From his reclining position, the Indiaman regarded her with great interest. "Good, I am ready to improve—I am bored, with nothing to do. Did you know that the Abbot has a laboratory in the tower?"

Thoroughly annoyed, Lisabetta hissed, "Do not touch his precious machines, you fool—no faster way to be thrown out."

But the patient was unrepentant, and only shrugged. "There is no harm to reconnoitering the place—the Abbot does not suspect that I am feigning.

In fact, we had a conversation about the Tamil Nadu Hospital, and he was very interested in what I could tell him. And he has offered to play chess with me, to help pass the time."

"Worse and worse." Lisabetta shut her eyes briefly, as she straightened up. "*Le bon Dieu* protect me from foolish men."

"I am not foolish," he said, stung. "But I am bored."

"Not much longer," she warned. "Stay sharp."

"I don't know that I was much needed, to begin with," he ventured. "This place does not seem very dangerous."

With all seriousness, she bent to straighten his coverlet and replied, "That is exactly why it is dangerous, *mon ami*—because it does not seem so. You must trust your master—he knows what he is about."

Hahn raised his brows as she tucked him in. "I am surprised that he trusts you."

"He *doesn't* trust me," she explained with some exasperation. "Fah, but you make far too many assumptions. Never assume that anyone is what they seem, and above all, stay sharp—you will live longer."

"I don't want to live longer," he groused. "I am ready to die from boredom."

"Not if I strangle you first," she threatened.

With a gleam, he replied, "Ah—now, there is a glimpse of what I was warned."

"What were you warned?" she asked, thinking that he was foolish enough to tell her.

"I was warned that I must not be beguiled—that you may be beautiful, but you are very dangerous."

"*Enfin*, it is very good advice," she agreed. "Only you have not taken it, since you tell it to me freely—fah, but there is little hope for you."

"When is the girl coming?"

"Soon," she instructed. "Remember your orders, and *pour l'amour du ciel*, do not dally with the Abbot."

With a gleam, he suggested, "Perhaps I should dally with you, instead."

But she only pronounced with some approval, "Better; a flirtation might help to lower my guard—but you should have made the attempt immediately."

"I learn at your feet," he replied solemnly, and she gave him one last, chiding look before she walked away.

Forcing her steps to be unhurried, she made her way over to Sebastian's chamber, and—after closing the door behind her—made a worried assessment of the still, wan figure that lay on the bed. "Are you sleeping, dearest?" she whispered, as she quietly pulled up the stool. "I have news."

There was no response, and with a panicked pang of alarm, Lisabetta grasped her sister's hand, only to find that is was blessedly warm—*merci le bon Dieu*.

At her touch, Eugenie struggled to open her eyes, the blue veins in her eyelids stark against the paleness of her skin. "Betta," she breathed, and attempted a smile as her eyes fluttered open. "How good to see you."

Lisabetta mustered her warmest smile. "I have wonderful news, dearest. Angelique is coming for a visit—tomorrow. She will be in this very room with you, and she will show you her dolls."

But her sister only frowned, and plucked at the coverlet with her stick-thin fingers. "Please—there is no need, Betta, although I know you mean well. I am a sick stranger; I will only frighten her."

"Nonsense; I will tell her that you are an angel on the mend." With some emphasis, Lisabetta added, "Because you are on the mend, my darling; Julian is concocting a new potion as we speak, and he has high hopes."

"Oh? He did not make mention, this morning."

"He thinks you are doing very well, dearest. And he thinks the new tincture will help give you strength."

"I would love to see Angelique," Eugenie admitted. "But what has happened, that you have no fears to bring her here?"

"Nothing," Lisabetta offered easily.

At her sister's skeptical expression, she confessed, "I've decided to bring her to stay at the Abbey."

Alarmed, the other young woman asked, "Georges is dead?"

"No—he is very much alive, but with Josephine dead, I think it will be safest for her to be here."

Thoughtfully, Eugenie searched her sister's face for a moment, before a glint of amusement appeared in her sunken eyes. "What is the gambit, Betta? And why don't you wish to tell me?"

"It is a very good gambit," Lisabetta confessed with a smile. "You will be amazed."

"Better than what we managed in Honfleur?"

"Perhaps, although that was one of our best. Remember how the Pasha tried to escape out the window, and tore his breeches?"

Eugenie smiled. "He wasn't fast enough; his wife shoved him headlong."

"Nothing less than what he deserved."

The two young women chuckled at the memory, and Lisabetta was much heartened to see a tinge of color appear in her sister's pale cheeks. "Shall I bring some soup? You must eat a bit, to prepare for Angelique's visit."

Her sister drew a breath, her thin chest rising and falling. "If you insist—I haven't much of an appetite."

"Well, Julian will bring his new potion soon, and you must have something at hand to take away the taste."

"Very well, then."

"And we must clear a space for Angelique's dollhouse, Genie; Georges made it for her—it is a sight to behold."

Eugenie smiled softly. "We had a dollhouse, once."

"Yes, we did—thanks to Josephine."

Her sister closed her eyes, and whispered, "I

dream about it, sometimes—dream about when we were little, and playing in the garden."

"There is no time to dream," Lisabetta said firmly, and stood to run her hands briskly down her sister's arms. "I will call for soup and more pillows—you will need to sit up, if you are going to play with Angelique."

After a moment, Eugenie opened her eyes again. "Very well, dearest."

CHAPTER 22

To her proctor's surprise, Lisabetta ordered soup and pillows, and then retreated back into Sebastian's chamber for an hour before she emerged again, briskly informing him that she needed to speak with the Director.

"He is in the tower," the man ventured, giving her a significant look. "I am not certain he would like to be disturbed."

"It can't wait," she said, and brushed by him. "I'm going up."

"Oh—oh, but mademoiselle—"

And so, Lisabetta lifted up her skirts and hurried up the ancient, winding steps to the laboratory room at its top. The door was locked, of course, but she hammered on it with the heel of her hand. "Open up, Julian; it's me—I'm alone."

Almost immediately the heavy door swung open, and she was confronted by a worried Julian, dressed in his shirtsleeves. "What is it? Sebastian?"

Without preamble, she began, "You need to give Eugenie something—I told her that you were concocting a new potion."

There was a small pause, and then he pulled her gently in to close the door behind her, and led her over to sit upon the stool he'd just vacated. "I am afraid there is little hope, my dear."

Impatiently, she sprang up again, brushing away tears with the back of her hand and rather surprised to discover that she was weeping. "You must *do* something—she must live for just a bit longer, Julian. It is—oh, it is so very important."

In the same gentle tone, he explained, "I run a risk, in that anything I give her may do more harm than good. Her heart is very weak."

"You must *do* something—she mustn't lose hope, she mustn't—mustn't die, not yet." She paused, making a mighty effort to calm herself, and then added, "I am going to bring Angelique into her room, so that she can spend time with her—it will hearten her, I think."

In some surprise, he raised his brows. "I cannot fault you for wishing to do so, but if Eugenie is Sebastian, it will raise a few questions."

But Lisabetta found that she was having trouble controlling the quaver in her voice. "It doesn't *matter* anymore, Julian—none of it matters anymore—can't you see? The only thing that matters is that she lives just a little bit longer." Pausing to press her trembling lips together, she then asked rather angrily, "So—will you do as I ask, or won't you?"

He laid soothing hands on her upper arms. "Of course, I will. I will do whatever you wish."

But the sincere timbre of his voice only had the opposite effect, as she began to sob—taking huge, shuddering breaths, and unable to control herself. "Oh—oh Julian—you have been so good—so good to us—"

Her shoulders heaving, she couldn't finish the sentence, and he carefully folded her into his arms as though she were a child, and held her close against him. "Hush, now," he murmured against her head. "It is up to us to show your sister that she has nothing to fear—yes?"

Catching her breath on a sob, she nodded. "Yes—yes, I know. I'm the one who's afraid—not Eugenie."

"What is this?" he teased gently. "What has happened to my fearless Lisabetta?"

"I am not fearless," she admitted, drawing a deep breath so as to control herself. "I am so very afraid that she is going to die too soon."

He bent his head to search her eyes. "Too soon for what?"

She avoided his gaze, and hid her face in his shirtfront, instead. "I cannot tell you—you would be horrified."

"My dear," he remonstrated gently. "You know better than to think such a thing. Can't you tell me?"

"I am running the greatest gambit I have ever run," she whispered.

"Yes—for the Englishman."

But she shook her head slightly. "No. For Angelique. And for you."

There was a small pause, and she could sense his surprise. "But you cannot tell me what it is?"

"No," she replied. "It is truly shocking, Julian. And you are far too honorable."

"I see," he replied thoughtfully, his voice reverberating in his chest, under her cheek. "In that case, I think we must marry."

She paused, blinking, and then slowly drew back to stare up at him in disbelief. "*What?*"

Seeing her surprise, he smiled slightly, and brushed a tendril of hair back from her face with gentle fingers. "If you can't tell me whatever it is, I must assume the worst, and you will need my support."

Astonished, she brushed her cheeks again with the back of her hand. "*Sainte Mère de Dieu*, but I should have gone hysterical long before now."

"I will ask the Hospitaller to marry us immediately, in the Chapel."

But she only closed her eyes in chagrin. "I cannot marry—not quite yet. And there is the small matter of my betrothal to the Baron Corvairre."

His brows drew down. "*What?*"

She explained, "It seemed the best tack to take, so that the King will be allayed—so that everyone will be allayed—and so that Eugenie and I are no longer at risk."

He continued to stare at her incredulously. "But surely, you do not intend to marry him?"

"No—I will never marry anyone, save you."

Thinking this over, he pulled her into an embrace again, his palms moving gently along her back. "Then we will marry in secret. No one need know, unless it becomes necessary. And that way, if anyone attempts a forced marriage, it will be null and void."

With a small sigh, she rested within the circle of his arms—*tiens*, but it felt better than she'd even imagined—a shame, that she had to ruin this much longed-for moment. "I cannot marry—not yet."

He was silent for a moment, coming to the obvious conclusion. "You do not trust me with the treasure."

"Of course, I do; I trust you with my life—with all of our lives. Never fear, Julian, we will marry." She glanced up at him. "And then we will move to Gottingen."

There was a small silence, whilst his hands continued to move gently on her back—it seemed he was reluctant to let her go, now that he'd finally taken hold of her. "I cannot go to Gottingen; I am needed here."

"No," she replied in a firm tone. "We will allow someone else to sort-out the next war—we've done enough. And a fresh start in a different country would avoid all awkward explanations as to why the Abbot of Beaulieu has married a baseborn woman of questionable virtue."

"Because he loves her," he replied. "He always has."

"Oh," she breathed, fresh tears filling her eyes as

she leaned back to gaze up at him. "I love you too—I always have, too."

She ran a hand across his chest and lifted her face for his kiss—after all, the poor man needed some prompting as to how to go about such things—but found, to her deep disappointment, that instead of responding to this invitation he rather firmly set her at arm's length.

"Not until we are married," he said.

They regarded each other as Lisabetta's mouth twisted in amusement. "This is a very good gambit," she acknowledged. "Even though I may be forgiven for thinking that you long for my treasure more than you long for me."

"If I am to be your husband, I would like to know what it is that you are planning," he countered in a level tone.

"Not as yet—whether or not you withhold your favors," she replied, just as firmly. "Which reminds me, I am slated to go out walking with the Englishman at any minute—he is courting me too, remember."

He couldn't help but smile at this absurdity, and ran a distracted hand over his face. "What in heaven's name do you hope to accomplish, Lisabetta?"

She was amused, herself—truly, she felt remarkably light-hearted and a bit giddy, despite the cataclysmic events that were unfolding. "Do not invoke heaven; they may not approve of my methods."

But he would not be distracted and persisted, "Why are you allied with the Englishman? You must know that you risk yourself—he could force you to marry him, and he now he has the means to do so." He paused, and then revealed, "I am fairly certain he knows of Eugenie, which is why his man is posted here."

With a little sigh, she confessed, "I am the one who told him of Eugenie, and I am the one who insisted that his man be posted."

He stared at her in surprised silence for a moment, and who could blame him? Together, they'd taken drastic measures to hide Eugenie—and the child she'd borne. "Yet, you cannot tell me why?"

Carefully, she explained, "You are constrained, Julian—constrained by what has happened to your poor Order, and who you are now answerable to."

But he only shook his head, adamantly. "I would never betray your sister."

"No, of course not, but—" here, she paused, trying to think of the best way to put it "—you and I tend to look at means-to-an-end from a different perspective."

"You promised me," he said rather heavily, "that no one else would be murdered."

"No more murders," she assured him, and hoped that this was true. "I will take no chances—remember that I have worked alongside these people for years, and know exactly how ruthless they can be. But I've also learned that alliances are constantly shifting—depending upon which way the wind blows—and that such a thing may be turned to one's advantage. If the incentive is there, enemies will turn in an instant and work together for a common goal."

Implacably, he insisted, "The Englishman is an enemy of my Church, Lisabetta. At the Congress, Castlereagh is working very hard to restrict her power."

But she shook her head. "No—the Englishman cares only about his country. Trust me on this; if his mad King decreed them all Roman Catholics again, he would go to Mass without batting an eyelash."

Bemused, he regarded her in silence.

"It is true," she insisted. "I know him as well as anyone can, I think."

"Even if that is true, what common goals do we share? I will not work for England, Lisabetta."

"Never say never," she smiled. "You will be astonished, *mon Abbé*; we will hold our own private Congress."

CHAPTER 23

*I*t had already been a very eventful day, but Lisabetta mentally girded her loins to go walking with the Englishman along the Abbey's perimeter pathway, even though it was drizzling rain. She needed to have her wits about her; one had to be very careful about what one said to the Englishman.

They greeted each other courteously in the foyer, and then walked out to admire the view—obscured a bit, by the clouds. Ostensibly, he'd came alone, but Lisabetta knew that he had a protective detail with him; he was an excellent planner, and one who took no chances—which was exactly the reason she'd enlisted him in her gambit.

"Is Tremaine about?" she asked, glancing over toward the trees as they began their walk. Even though she was well-versed in spotting such things, she could see no hint of those who watched them.

"I am not at liberty to say," he replied easily.

She shrugged, unconcerned. "Fah—no need to be so cagey. I only wished to say hello—I have fond memories."

Tremaine was a young man who'd worked as an operative for the Englishman in a few earlier adventures, and he'd been thrown her way in the obvious hope she'd become romantically involved, and reveal information. Because she'd played all sides in the war, she tended to be the keeper of quite a few secrets.

Lisabetta, however, knew the value of the secrets she kept, and had easily sidestepped this lure. Indeed, the fact that the Englishman had not known, back then, who it was that truly held her heart only proved how well she did keep her secrets.

He offered, "I will send Tremaine your regards."

"How does he?" she asked in a neutral tone.

There was a small silence. "Not as well as he should."

This was a rare moment of honesty; Tremaine was clever, loyal and a good man, but he tended to drink to excess, and Lisabetta knew that he'd been relegated to the back lists, because of it—she imagined that it was the very reason he was now on the Englishman's protective detail, rather that running his own gambit, somewhere. This deadly business they engaged in had no place for someone with a weakness to exploit; it was a shame, but she understood it better than most.

She made no response—he'd probably told her more than he should, and so she wouldn't ask him to enlarge on the subject. After a moment, the Englishman suggested, "If you think it would be helpful, I can send Tremaine to call upon you at the Abbey. Another ardent suitor might turn the trick."

"Not at all necessary," she replied, with a small smile.

Hearing the nuance in her tone, he glanced at her, a speculative light in his eye. "Oh? How goes the war?"

"Surprisingly well; the Abbot of Beaulieu has proposed marriage this very day."

He chuckled—unusual, in that he was one who rarely laughed. "Has he? You amaze me."

"I amaze myself," she admitted. "I think it helped matters that you proposed first, and that he doesn't like you very much."

"Which fell-in with your theory. Well-played."

But she shook her head slightly. "It was only possible to begin with because he watches the world changing, and longs to be a part of it—I know him well, you see."

"Then I must envy him," the spymaster offered gallantly.

She made a wry mouth. "Prettily said, but you are thanking *le bon Dieu* that it is not you who stands in his shoes."

Nodding thoughtfully, he admitted, "Perhaps; you and I are both very strong-willed, which would not bode well for a marriage. But you must have a care; the moment you marry your Abbot, his Order will have control of your riches."

"Oh, I am well-aware, and it is of all things ironic; Julian has come around too soon, and now he is astonished that I wish to keep him at arm's length."

He glanced at her, the grey eyes keen. "I can only hope that you do not deal with him the same way you dealt with the Count Vassily."

"You can only hope," she agreed, unruffled; it was not a surprise that he was aware of the circumstances of the Count's death.

In an even tone, he continued, "Are you going to tell me why you thought that was necessary?"

"No," she replied, just as evenly. "I am not."

But he persisted, "Vassily was the Tsar's man first, Lisabetta, even though he was a Knight. I cannot think you wish to invite the Tsar's scrutiny into these matters."

But she was unrepentant. "On the contrary, I welcome the Tsar's scrutiny; it will only bring more pressure to bear on our target."

He thought about this, as they walked along. "Perhaps. However, in the future I would ask to be consulted before such a drastic step is taken."

"Perhaps I should consult Rochon, also," she replied a bit tartly. "I hear rumors that his wings have been clipped." This, to remind him that he hadn't been forthcoming with her, either.

"I can neither confirm nor deny," her companion replied, unrepentant. "And in any event, you must not forget the fisherman; he could easily step-up into a more substantial role, in Rochon's absence."

"Oh, I do not forget the fisherman; I held my blade to his throat this very morning."

The Englishman was seen to close his eyes, briefly.

"He was trying to cheat me," she defended herself. "It would have seemed strange, if I'd allowed him to."

"Be that as it may, if you would take no further such actions without consulting me first, please."

"*Certainment*," she agreed, even though they both knew that such an agreement meant little, in their world.

"On the other hand, I am hopeful that the news of the Count's disappearance will not get to the Tsar before our business here is completed."

She raised her brows with keen interest. "Oh? Does the delegation approach?"

"The delegation from Vienna approaches," he announced with a small, satisfied smile. "In stealth and trepidation."

She laughed aloud. "*Tiens*, but this is a well-thought out plan, and worth every penny that you wrest from me."

"At the risk of being indelicate, I will point out that the emerald you gave me was paste."

But she only smiled. "Of course, it was—I had yet to see if you would hold faith, and you have. Here is the genuine one, with my compliments." She stumbled a bit, and placed a hand on his arm as though to steady herself, and he placed his own hand over hers for a moment, as though to aid her.

She regained her footing, and they continued on, walking side-by-side. He remarked, "The fake was quite good."

"Yes; I made the acquaintance of a gypsy engraver, once."

"I know the very one—a talented fellow."

They'd completed their circuit, and as they began to turn back, Lisabetta asked, "Did you manage to extract a personal item from our target?"

"His rosary," the grey-eyed man disclosed. "Which his mother gave him."

In all admiration, she stared at him. "Oh-ho, that is very well done—how did you manage it?"

"Hahn," he replied. "Hahn is very adept at infiltration."

She warned, "He's a bit rash, though; have a care where you use him."

"Good advice," her companion replied, in a non-committal tone.

"Where is the rosary now? How will you get it to me?"

"It rests under your pillow," he replied. "Thanks to Hahn."

She laughed aloud. "*C'est bien*. Is there anything I should know, now that the *denouement* approaches? Hahn will give you entry into the Abbey?"

"Yes. I will come alone so as to raise no fears, but I will have reinforcements watching from the river, in the event anything goes awry. The signal will be a swinging lantern out a high window."

She smiled ironically. "If anything goes awry, rescue from the river will be the least of our worries."

"I can only hope we do not light the spark for the next war," he agreed. "But I have every confidence, now that events are unfolding. I will confess I was not certain that the target would take the bait."

She shrugged. "You do not know the players as well as I do."

"Undoubtedly true; *brava*, for putting it all together."

But she only demurred, "It comes of gathering up bits and pieces, and then using them to my advantage."

"Yes," he agreed. "But that is a talent, in and of itself. I will miss you, Lisabetta; you are a bright spot in my rather dreary world."

But she only made a face. "Fah, I will not miss any of this—not at all; I am sick to the teeth of intrigue. The only intrigue I wish from now on is what to make for dinner, and whether the baby has the croup."

He eyed her shrewdly. "Do you think you will be content with such a life? I am not so certain."

"I will never regret a single moment," she replied with complete certainty. "It is what I have longed for my whole life. You would not understand, because you have never been a stray-relation, and always dependent upon the grace of others."

"I would think—having been the recipient of Josephine's grace—that you have little to complain about."

"Yes—I was lucky, but it only proves my point. This world is an unforgiving one, when it comes to those who have fallen into sin."

He nodded. "And so, you will marry honorably."

"I am not the only one who will marry honorably," she reminded him with twinkle.

He gave her a dubious glance. "That remains to be seen; it would be along the lines of a miracle."

"Fortune favors the bold," she reminded him.

CHAPTER 24

Lisabetta was not very surprised when the proctor knocked on the door of the women's quarters rather early the next morning, to inform her that the Director was without, and inquiring as to whether she would like to review the garden so as to plan the spring planting.

With a sigh, Lisabetta brushed her hair and braided it with quick hands, trying to decide what to tell Julian and what not to tell him. A shame, that the man couldn't be taken into her confidence—not as yet, anyway—but he was honest to a fault, and so she'd best be careful.

Swinging her cloak around her shoulders, she stepped out onto the pathway and smiled at him, where he waited at the garden gate. And here is my inspiration, she thought to herself; if all comes to pass as planned, I will be waking up every single morning to the sight of this wonderful, wonderful man.

"Good morning, *mon Abbé*."

He bowed his head in greeting, but she was not fooled; he was unhappy with her, yet again—which undoubtedly meant he'd become aware of the delegation from Vienna. Ah, well; she'd hoped for the element of surprise, but it was not to be. Best soothe his alarm as well as she was able.

She fell into step beside him, and teased, "If you continue to meet with me unchaperoned, tongues will start wagging."

"When we marry, they will cease."

Unable to help herself, she cast him a delighted smile; it was a wonderful thing, to hear him mention their marriage as a certainty—especially considering the alarming reports he must be hearing. "You mustn't worry, Julian; I will be a pattern-card of respectability when we set-up our new home. You deserve no less."

"I will always love you, Lisabetta; you needn't think you must change for me."

Again, she was absurdly gratified that yesterday's proposal hadn't been retracted in light of more recent events. "Nevertheless, you will be astonished—I will be staider than the staidest hausfrau in Gottingen."

He contemplated the pathway ahead, as they walked along, and chose his words carefully. "You have survived these past few years only because you excel in dishonesty; it may be a hard habit to break."

"Fah," she declared; "I will break all my bad habits and stamp them into pieces on the floor. I will regenerate, just like the little cells that you watch under your microscope. My promise, Julian."

He was silent for a moment, and so she ventured, "Tell me what you have heard, my husband-to-be, so that I may soothe you as best I can."

"I have heard that Tallyrand, himself, is traveling in this direction, and taking care not to be recognized."

"Yes," she affirmed.

It seemed clear he was surprised by her admission. "Why?"

In an apologetic tone, she repeated, "I cannot tell you, Julian—not yet."

With a frown, he continued, "I cannot think it is a coincidence, that Tallyrand approaches just as Angelique has been moved into the Abbey, and the Englishman posts his man on-site. Surely you can understand why I am concerned; you seem to be risking Angelique as well as my Order's work."

"Hahn has guarded Eugenie these past few weeks —that is why he is posted outside her door," she explained. "With Josephine's death, she was more at risk than ever—and she is vulnerable, whereas I am not."

Frowning, he turned to meet her eyes. "Surely, you had only to ask—I would have posted my own man as guard, and then the Abbey would not have an outsider, posted within."

Her expression as serious as his own, she explained, "You have done what you could, Julian, but your Order has been dispossessed, and the

Knights must rely on the Tsar to survive. We saw this with the Count Vassily—it is no coincidence, that he sought Eugenie's whereabouts immediately after Josephine's death; a death that occurred just as the Tsar was visiting her."

He was silent for a few steps, and then admitted, "It is indeed troubling, but there have been no accusations of foul play."

She made a face. "Who would dare, with the Congress ongoing? It is an unfortunate chain of events, you must admit; and so, I have colluded with the Englishman so that you would not be put in the position of having to choose between us and your Order."

He fell silent again, and she was sympathetic; Julian's Order needed to survive for the greater good, but its survival was now dependent upon the grace of the Tsar of Russia, who had his own rapacious agenda. It was a terrible dilemma.

She offered, "I will bring no harm to your Order, nor will I interfere with its work. I swear it on my soul, Julian."

He glanced at her. "Then are you trying to force Tallyrand to publicly acknowledge Angelique? Is that your aim?"

"Something like that," she hedged.

He frowned in confusion. "But we have discussed this; if he acknowledges her, he may well decide to remove her to his estate and none of us could prevent it. He remains a powerful man—especially with the negotiations ongoing—and no one dares to cross him."

"He will not seize Angelique," she assured him. "Do you see? It is one of the reasons I enlisted the Englishman."

Thinking his over, he nodded; Tallyrand had to curry favor with the British—at the present time, anyway—because he was secretly aligned with them against Russia, and he dared not take the chance that this interesting bit of information might be exposed at the negotiating table in Vienna.

Julian continued, "So; the Englishman has leverage over Tallyrand—this is true. But can you trust the Englishman to hold faith? Why would he do so—why would he come here himself, and risk his own men so as to force Tallyrand to acknowledge Angelique?"

"He is getting paid to do so," she reminded him. "Or, he will be paid, as soon as the gambit is accomplished."

But her betrothed was far too clever to buy this explanation, and gave her a look. "This makes little sense to me, Lisabetta; the Englishman has far more pressing matters to attend to, no matter how much of the treasure you've promised him."

"I know it doesn't make sense," she conceded. "Suffice it to say that the Englishman's goals align with mine, in this gambit."

"And you trust him?" The tone of his voice held a hint of incredulity.

"In this, I do." Carefully, she offered, "Everyone has leverage over everyone else."

He couldn't help but smile. "Then it does indeed sound like the Congress."

"All will be well," she promised. "But you mustn't do anything to alarm Tallyrand, or to betray his presence, here—he must be able to come and go with none the wiser."

He shook his head in wonder. "How was Tallyrand persuaded to come here, away from the Congress?"

This was, of course, a valid question, since the exposure of one more illegitimate child amongst the many would not have made much difference to the notorious minister. Vaguely, Lisabetta replied, "He comes because he has heard a few disturbing rumors that he cannot like."

He drew a long breath, and gazed up over the hedges. "I think it is you, who out-spies the rest of us."

But she demurred, "I am no spy—I've never been. But I pay close attention to what others say and do—especially when what they say does not match what they do."

They walked for a few more steps, and then he asked, "If I am kept unaware, aren't you worried that I will upend your gambit, all unknowing?"

"That is unlikely," she replied. "The gambit assumes that everyone will behave in a predictable manner, including you."

He nodded. "You knew that I would eavesdrop

on the Englishman's proposal, and that I would be very unhappy about it."

Hedging, she ventured, "Perhaps."

"I cannot like the idea that he conspired with you against me, Lisabetta."

"You won't change your mind, will you?" she pleaded. "I needed to do something drastic, Julian—you are so stubborn."

He blew out a breath. "I think 'drastic' does not even begin to describe the situation. But I suppose—in this one instance—the ends do justify the means."

Thoroughly relieved, she promised, "Just wait until we are abed, and you will never doubt it again."

Surreptitiously, his hand came to rest for a lingering moment on her lower back. "We should marry immediately, then—so that I may test your powers of persuasion."

"And there's your leverage over me," she sighed. "I am *longing* to take you to bed."

"Then we should marry; you may freely give the Englishman his treasure as promised—my oath on it," he offered. "No one need know that we marry, and it would be an extra layer of protection for you. I may be forced to answer to the Tsar—this is true; but the Englishman, in turn, must placate the Tsar."

"Everyone has leverage over everyone else," she repeated. "When we marry, some of it will disappear, and I can't allow that to happen. It is the beauty of the gambit, and why it will work."

Ceding this point, he nevertheless cautioned, "No matter how well you have planned your gambit,

Tallyrand is not one who will like to have his hand forced—I doubt he will be as predictable as you believe."

"You will see; and I will marry you a thousand times over, *mon Abbé*—only not just yet." Deciding to change the subject, she asked, "How does Sebastian, this morning?"

"I have given him a feverfew tincture; it is an appetite stimulant, but it must be balanced against the danger to his heart. He did seem a bit recovered this morning, and asked if I knew about the child's coming visit."

Relieved, she nodded. "Good. We must keep him alive at all costs."

"Whatever God wills," he reminded her.

"*Certainment*," she agreed. "And we are fortunate that God has willed us your tincture."

CHAPTER 25

*A*fter her walk, Lisabetta returned to the women's quarters and hung her cloak back on its hook. In the same way that she'd not been surprised to see Julian this morning, she was not surprised to see that the proctor was crouched in her little sitting room, and stoking the fire in the hearth.

"Thank you, monsieur," she said politely. "It is cold this morning—*peste*, I will miss the beauty of this place, but I will not miss the weather for one moment."

Her companion sat back on his haunches, and offered a dry little smile. "Will you return to Spain, mademoiselle?"

"Portugal, instead. It is marvelously sunny in Portugal." She removed her gloves, and bent to warm her hands at the fire.

"What did he wish to see you about?"

She quirked her mouth. "He asks what the Englishman said to me, during his visit yesterday."

The little man eyed her sidelong. "I am curious about this, also."

"The Englishman seeks to marry my treasure," she revealed. As does *Monsieur le Abbé.*"

The proctor's brows drew down in incredulity. "But—but *surely*, the Abbot cannot marry? He is a priest."

"Apparently, you are mistaken. And he seeks to marry me before the Englishmen has the chance. I have soothed them both, but I may have to leave before matters become heated."

Again, the proctor frowned. "The Abbot would defy the Englishman? Is he mad?"

But Lisabetta only warned, "The Abbot must never be underestimated; I have known him all my life."

Her companion stared into the flames, clearly made uneasy by these revelations. "Perhaps the Abbot should meet with an accident; it would be an easy thing, here along the cliffs."

She thought this over for a moment, but then shook her head. "We mustn't overreact; the plan is so well-advanced that there is little the Abbot can do to upset it." She paused, and then added in a practical manner, "And in the end, he has little choice. He must obey his Order, and his Order must obey your master."

The proctor nodded, as he continued his perusal of the fire. "This is true. Although it makes me uneasy, to learn that he is not truly a priest."

"It was a surprise," she agreed. "Have you heard from your master?"

He nodded briskly, and turned to face her. "My master sends his great appreciation, and looks forward to hearing that we have accomplished his aims." He paused. "My master seeks more gold, if you can manage it."

She made a wry mouth. "Of course, he does; if he hopes to seize the whole of Prussia, he must spread more bribes around the Congress."

A bit primly, the man answered, "I ask no questions, mademoiselle."

Absently rubbing her hands, she replied, "You should, you know; you never know what you might find out. Did you know that Gottingen is in Prussia?"

He frowned at her, bemused. "Gottingen, mademoiselle?"

She nodded. "Yes—it is a city in Hanover."

Her companion ventured, "Is this important, mademoiselle?"

"It is, to me," she replied.

But the Proctor would not be distracted from the subject at hand. "Could you deliver the gold today, mademoiselle? I am told that time is of the essence."

"Very well—I must be discreet, though; the remainder of the treasure cannot disappear all at once, or the sharp-eyed Abbot may notice." She glanced at her companion with a hint of humor. "And I will need my own bribe too—you mustn't forget."

The little man hastened to assure her, "My master promises to pay you as before."

"Good." Straightening up, she sighed. "I will be happy when the Congress is over. I am weary of toting a heavy basket down the hill."

"Georges is a good man," the Proctor declared. "He whittled a whistle for me."

"Did he?" She smiled. "Yes, he is a good man."

"A shame, that his wife died—quite a surprise; she wasn't very old."

"He will miss her sorely," she agreed. "But I imagine he will find another—he is well set-up, and now he has even more riches, thanks to your master." As though suddenly struck, she asked, "Have we heard from the Count Vassily?"

With an annoyed frown, her companion replied, "We have not, mademoiselle. It is very strange—unlikely that he would double-deal, considering his holdings in St. Petersburg."

"You never know who you can trust," she advised. "And so, perhaps you must find a new contact."

"I, myself, will make the deliveries for the time being, mademoiselle."

Lisabetta feigned surprise. "Will you? That is very good of you—I hope your faithfulness will be rewarded, you've stayed far longer than you thought."

Preening a bit, the proctor nodded in acknowledgement. "It has not been a hardship, in truth. I am happy to serve my master, and I don't mind it here, mademoiselle—it is a lot like home."

She made a face. "Your home country is too cold, too—as Napoleon himself discovered."

Her companion made a derisive sound. "Bah—he was a stupid fool, and his comeuppance came far too late."

But Lisabetta gently reminded him, "He should never be discounted, my friend. His followers are devoted, and chafing for the chance to bring him back into power."

"He has few followers, anymore," the man declared with some satisfaction. "My master is a hero, for defeating him so soundly."

"Your master is a very wise man," she agreed. "I must go; the chickens are calling."

He chuckled. "Not much longer, mademoiselle."

"No," she agreed. "Not much longer."

CHAPTER 26

After donning her work-apron, Lisabetta crossed the barnyard toward the chicken coop—she was a bit late, due to Julian's visit, and so the wretched birds would be hungry. This was immediately confirmed when she opened the coop, and the chickens started a raucous squawking, flapping their wings and stepping on each other in their haste to get through the door.

After scooping up a bowl of chicken-feed from the burlap sack, she then went outside to begin idly tossing it onto the hard-packed ground—much to the delight of the chickens, as they frantically converged on their meal.

Whilst the birds were thus engaged, she went into the coop to collect the morning's eggs—the general commotion outside obscuring the strange fact that some of the chickens continued to peacefully roost, and showed not the slightest bit of interest in their breakfast, outside. With a quick glance at the courtyard—which was deserted at this hour, save for the chickens—Lisabetta quickly slipped a hand into a small opening hidden amongst the feathers on one chicken's back, and pulled forth a small packet—jewels that had been wrapped and carefully secreted inside the stuffed chickens.

The original Abbot—Dom Nicolas—had decided that the St. Alban's treasure was best hidden by dispersal in unusual hiding places, and had tasked the young Julian with seeing to it. Julian had then used the new taxidermy techniques to place stuffed chickens amongst the living, so that they could secret packets containing a few gemstones or coins within the dead birds, and thus have easy access to small portions of the treasure.

In a similar deception, gold ingots were painted to appear as iron, and were then incorporated into the structure of the roost and the nesting boxes. The lion's share of the treasure, however, was buried beneath the coop, with the trapdoor to the chamber covered by straw and chicken droppings. On occasion, Georges would access the underground chamber under the guise of having been hired to clean-out the coop, and he would thus replenish that which had been removed from the stuffed chickens and the roosting structure.

It was a clever contrivance; if anyone managed to trace the missing treasure to the Abbey, they would naturally look to the Abbey's strong-room, which was well-fortified and not easy to breach. If they nonetheless managed to break-in and steal the wooden caskets, they would find that they only contained iron bars painted to appear as gold, and paste-work gems, courtesy of the gypsy engraver. The presumption would thus be that it was all a ruse to make it appear that the treasure was stored at the Abbey when it was not; no one would think for a moment that the priceless St. Alban's treasure abided under the chicken coop's messy floor.

The treasure had been vastly depleted over the years—and with good cause; the secret network of Knights that continued to operate on the Continent had to be supported, somehow. Due to Napoleon's prohibition, the Order had been unable to seek funding from the public or from the Vatican, and so much of the St. Alban's treasure had been used to allow them to continue their work—serving the destitute poor and freeing as many slaves as possible, by escape on chartered ships or by outright purchase.

Neither Lisabetta or Eugenie had any objection to such a use; their father had conspired with Dom Nicolas to secret the treasure at the Abbey, and then a portion of it had been bartered to allow for their own survival—if some would also be bartered to allow for the Order's survival, that only seemed fair. To Lisabetta's mind, the situation was very similar to that of a courtesan who'd saved-up her jewels in anticipation of leaner times; the ancient St. Alban's monks—one would think—would heartily approve of how their treasure-trove had been used to support their Church, during some very lean times indeed.

After Lisabetta's egg-basket was laden with eggs

—the jewels and two gold ingots hidden beneath them—she carefully set it down to wash her hands at the pump. Julian had explained that it was important to wash one's hands after touching the chickens—something having to do with his cell theory—and so she complied, mainly so as to humor him. He loved his work, loved his experiments, and loved his God; she may not feel as strongly about any of the three, but she definitely loved him. And by dint of patience, hard work, and a bit of listening at doors she'd managed to put together a plan to give him the life he'd always wanted, but dared not admit to. *S'il plaît à Dieu*, at least; she would very soon see if all her planning was to bear fruit.

After drying her hands on her apron, she lifted the basket and headed in a leisurely pace back toward the women's quarters. The waiting proctor received her parcel and then departed—with a self-important air—for Strasbourg, where he would pass it along to the next contact.

Lisabetta leaned in the doorway and watched him go; he was not often away from the premises, but it was important that he be absent when Angelique was transferred to the Abbey. If all went well, the poor man would return to find a surprising change in the situation—and with his master suddenly at a distinct disadvantage.

CHAPTER 27

That evening, Lisabetta visited Sebastian openly, without the restraint of having to hoodwink her proctor. Soon—*merci le bon Dieu*—the pretense would no longer be necessary, and if Julian thought her sister was well enough, they could move her sickbed to a more cheerful place—perhaps Georges house, where she could sit outside in the yard.

It was almost too much to be hoped—that things would turn out so well—and so Lisabetta tempered her expectations and instead was gratified by Eugenie's brighter eye; as had been hoped, the sick woman was much heartened by Angelique's coming visit, and was forcing herself to eat.

Closing the chamber door behind her, Lisabetta approached Hahn and instructed, "It is time to rise from your sickbed, *mon ami*; the girl will be here shortly. No one enters Sebastian's room without my permission, and above all, no one takes the girl anywhere without my permission."

"What about the Hospitaller?" he asked, as he stretched his arms over his head.

"Trust no one," she emphasized, a bit impatiently.

In an innocent tone, he slid his gaze toward her. "Not even the Director?"

Lisabetta closed her eyes, briefly. "No. But be assured, the Director is not going to take the girl anywhere without my permission."

"Right." In a bland tone, he offered, "It seems to me that you have a great influence over the Director. It is somewhat surprising."

But rather than be discomfited by this insinuation, Lisabetta only smiled upon him in approval. "*Tiens*, there is hope for you yet. In this business it is important—more important than anything else, perhaps—to watch interactions, and decide for yourself who is aligned and who is not, regardless of what you are told."

He cocked his head. "This is good advice, but I note that you do not answer my question."

With some seriousness, she explained, "Because the second most important thing is to never give out information—not unless you are paid for it, and even then, you should be very careful about what you disclose. The people who survive in this business are the people who keep their mouths firmly closed, and give nothing away."

He grinned and bowed his head. "I have learned much from you."

"Indeed, you have; we can only hope you listened. You have a weapon?"

"I do."

"Good; we will see to it that you have the only one—although I do not anticipate any trouble; our visitor will not want to bring an entourage."

Hahn raised his brows in confusion. "The girl has an entourage?"

Ah, thought Lisabetta; the Englishman has decided that this fellow should not be fully informed—or at least, not yet. "No—I speak of another visitor who will arrive quietly, and probably at night." Briskly, she added, "Only remember your orders, and do not ask too many questions."

Despite this stricture, he asked in all curiosity, "Who is this other visitor?"

Making an impatient sound, she turned away without deigning to answer.

And so, a short time later, Lisabetta dropped to her knees to greet Angelique with a mighty hug, as the little girl was escorted by Georges into the infirmary.

"I am coming for a visit," Angelique informed her, chattering with some excitement. "The donkey had such long ears. Georges has brought my dollhouse."

"I should not have made it so heavy," the older man complained. "My back is broken."

Whilst Angelique giggled, Lisabetta directed, "Come along, dearest; I want you to meet someone. Georges, if you would bring her dolls?"

Georges raised his eyebrows. "The proctor is gone?"

"Off to Strasbourg," she announced with some satisfaction. "He should not return before tomorrow."

Thinking about this, Georges cocked his head. "Perhaps he should not return at all?"

With a smile, Lisabetta touched his arm. "Patience, my friend. He is useful, in that I can still feed him misinformation."

The older man sighed. "Some other time, then."

"We shall see," she hedged, remembering with some regret her promise to commit no further murders. "Now come, we will reunite Eugenie and Angelique; it has been a long time for them."

And so, Eugenie greeted her shy daughter as Lisabetta stood in the doorway and watched, Georges standing by her side and discreetly wiping tears from his eyes. And who could blame him? Eugenie was due for a small measure of happiness, after everything she'd endured—after everything they'd all endured.

Only now—now it was all coming to an end, with Eugenie soon to say her final farewells. It would be very strange for Lisabetta; even though they'd often been apart, the two sisters had always shared an unbreakable bond—as well as harrowing adventures that could never be recounted to anyone else. By their wits, they'd survived—along with a full measure of luck—but now Eugenie's adventuring life was coming to a close, with Lisabetta determined to retire from the lists, herself. It was just as well; adventuring would never be the same, without her sister.

CHAPTER 28

Georges set-up the dollhouse in the antechamber, and the little girl seemed content to play with her dolls and visit with Eugenie for the remainder of the day—Lisabetta taking her for the occasional walk, so that Eugenie could rest.

Julian did not visit them, and Lisabetta could only surmise that he was preparing for their illustrious visitor and seeing to the Abbey's security. She'd already noted that the three patients who remained in the infirmary seemed supremely uninterested in the little girl and Georges—not a surprise, since Julian had seen to it that any true patients had been discharged or moved elsewhere. But those Knights who were posing as beggars would remain—mainly because the Abbot was not going to allow his stronghold to be invaded for mysterious purposes, especially when it involved the Englishman.

Lisabetta was not about to make mention—she'd

dared enough, as it was—but she anticipated that the Englishman would not care for this arrangement, since it could be presumed that he well-knew those remaining behind were not ordinary beggars. It seemed certain they were heading for a confrontation, but she decided there was little she could do to prevent it; hopefully they would avoid open warfare.

The Hospitaller prepared an evening meal for Angelique and Eugenie, brought-in on a tray so that they could eat together, and Lisabetta dismissed Georges, her gaze meeting his with an unspoken message to stay alert. As the older man left through the infirmary door, Lisabetta noted that Dom Julian was making his own approach, down the hallway.

With a cheerful smile, she greeted him. "*Mon Abbé*; Mademoiselle Angelique is much enjoying her visit."

"Very good," he replied, although she noted that —as he came through the door—his quick glance assessed the beggars who remained in their beds. Addressing Hahn, he observed in a friendly tone, "You seem much-recovered, sir; I am so pleased."

"I do feel much better," Hahn offered, without a shred of shame.

"If you would take-up your post," Julian continued in a courteous tone, "Our visitor is arriving at the back entry."

"So soon?" asked Lisabetta in surprise. "*Tiens*, but he comes with all speed."

"Indeed. I imagine he will not wish to stand on

formality, and so I have offered to escort him directly to these rooms, if that meets with your approval."

"Yes; I thank you for the warning, monsieur."

"Not at all." The Abbot then addressed Hahn. "Sir? If you would take-up your post outside the door, I will fetch our visitor."

"Oh—oh, yes, of course," said Hahn, and moved aside so that Julian could pass by. As soon as the Abbot was out of earshot, however, the Indiaman shot Lisabetta a worried glance—his tone a bit grave, for once. "I do not think these others are what they seem. Are we certain they are not armed?"

"I am not going to confirm nor deny anything," she explained, as though speaking to a simpleton. "Fah, but you learn slowly."

With a self-conscious duck of his head, he made a gesture. "If you will excuse me for just a moment? I must use the jakes."

"Good," she pronounced with approval. "You cannot like the odds, and will try to signal to your master to be wary. It is not necessary, however; I would imagine he is already on-site, and as wary as he ever will be."

Hahn hesitated, clearly torn. "Why should I trust you?"

"You shouldn't," she replied. "But—on the other hand—you shouldn't be absent from your post when your master appears."

Hahn's brows drew together. "Promise me," he said in all seriousness, "that you do not set a trap."

Lisabetta laughed aloud. "You are so very amusing, monsieur."

But whatever Hahn's response was to be would not be heard, because their conversation was interrupted by the Abbot, who was seen to approach down the hallway toward the infirmary, his tall figure engaged in civil conversation a smaller, older man, who walked with a decided limp.

In abject surprise, Hahn watched their approach, and then whispered to Lisabetta, "Hold a moment; isn't that—"

"Monsieur Tallyrand," Lisabetta said to the visitor, as she greeted him with a deep curtesy.

"Mademoiselle de Grère," their visitor replied courteously. "How good it is to see you again."

CHAPTER 29

"If you would take-up your post, monsieur?" Julian said to Hahn, as the Indiaman stood motionless.

"Of course," Hahn replied, and—unable to resist a last, incredulous glance at Tallyrand—he quickly slipped outside the door, and closed it after him.

"May I offer a chair, monsieur?" Julian asked their visitor. "You have had a long journey."

"Not as yet," the minister replied. "I have heard some disturbing news, and I thought I should come immediately to assess the situation for myself. I wouldn't want to risk dear Eugenie and—and the child."

"Angelique," Lisabetta reminded him.

"Yes—of course. May I visit with her?"

"You may," Lisabetta offered, and gestured for him to follow her to the antechamber. "I am afraid you must prepare yourself, monsieur; Eugenie has been ill, and is but a thread of her former self."

"I am sorry to hear of it," he said gravely, and Lisabetta could swear the words were sincere, even though the man was notorious for his insincerity.

They opened the chamber's door and stepped within; the candle beside the bed illuminated Eugenie, propped up by pillows as she spoke with Angelique over their meal, the little girl's dolls arrayed alongside her in the bed.

"Why—Charles," Eugenie pronounced in astonishment. "How wonderful."

With the grace of a practiced diplomat, Tallyrand pulled up a stool next to Eugenie's bedside, and readily took her hand in his. "Eugenie, my dear; it does my heart good to see you again. Forgive me for not visiting more often."

"You have been busy," Eugenie replied with a smile. "I understand."

"And here is our Angelique," he continued in a hearty tone. "A beautiful child; she has the look of her mother, which is fortunate. And who are these charming ladies?"

As the little girl shyly introduced the dolls, Lisabetta retreated back to the doorway so as to give them some privacy; Eugenie was not in love with Tallyrand—never had been—but they'd been very fond, once upon a time.

Julian moved to stand beside her in the antechamber doorway, as they watched the interaction between the three. In a low voice, he asked, "Are you going to tell me how you managed this?"

After a moment's consideration, she decided that she may as well; if she was going to be married to the man, she'd best learn to trust him—which was no easy feat; she tended to trust no one.

"There was an ugly rumor going about that Angelique was conceived because monsieur forced himself on my sister," she explained quietly—no need to mention that she was the one who'd started the rumor. "And so, he became concerned that Darton—one of his former operatives—was telling tales about him to stir up mischief at the Congress; Castlereagh would seize any excuse to throw him out."

"I see."

She decided to add, "It didn't help matters that there was another rumor that the Count Vassily was killed at Tallyrand's behest, for attempting to look into the matter. If such a rumor reached the Tsar's ears, he would join Castlereagh in demanding that Tallyrand be banned from the Congress."

"Ah," her companion said, and Lisabetta decided she would not be at all surprised if he already was aware of all this, and had guessed that she was behind these alarming rumors.

His next words affirmed this, as he said, "You've been very busy, arranging matters so as to put Tallyrand in a double-bind. But to what end?"

"It is toward a very good end—you will see."

But he would not be put off any longer, and his manner became more serious. "I am not so certain,

Lisabetta; if it was a good end, you would have enlisted me in your gambit."

"I couldn't," she explained. "Your Order relies on the goodwill of the Tsar of Russia, and the Tsar of Russia will not be best pleased with what we will accomplish here."

He paused in surprise, and she waited for his next, inevitable question, but was spared by Hahn, as he opened the door to allow the grey-eyed man entry into the infirmary.

"You are supposed to seek my permission, before allowing anyone entry," Lisabetta reminded the Indiaman in exasperation.

"I do not work for you; I work for him," Hahn pointed out reasonably.

"You must never admit to such a thing," the Englishman rebuked him in a mild tone. "And I might suggest that you return to your post."

Hahn closed the door behind him, and there was a long moment of tension, as the Abbot and the Englishman regarded one another warily. Abruptly, the Englishman asked, "How quickly did you see through him, sir?"

There was a small pause, and then Julian replied, "Subterfuge may not be his strong suit. I think he is more adept at physical infiltration; indeed, he has been within the Abbey's strong-room."

As though he were truly contrite, the Englishman bowed his head. "My apologies, sir."

"No harm done," Julian replied evenly.

Fah, Julian is not happy with this one, Lisabetta

thought; hopefully they won't come to blows before the evening is over.

But this seemed to be a faint hope, as the Englishman took a glance at the beggars arrayed in their sickbeds, showing no interest in the newcomer. "I would ask that your men be cleared out; I anticipate a frank conversation, and we must assure privacy."

"I will respectfully decline your request."

There was a small pause, and then—with a touch more deference—the Englishman explained, "I regret that we have conspired in secret, but—given the nature of the goals we seek—it was necessary."

"Which goals are these?" Julian asked, in a deceptively mild tone.

Lisabetta braced herself, but the grey-eyed man seemed to think it over for a moment, and then disclosed, "My aim is to force him to include a provision in the Viennese treaty that forbids the practice of slavery."

Holding her breath, Lisabetta waited for Julian's reaction; whilst the Knights of Malta had been founded to fight slavery—and had a long history of doing so—the Russian economy was premised largely upon serf-labor, which was a very similar system. And now, the survival of Julian's Order depended on appeasing the Tsar—it was something of a double-bind for him, too, with his worldly and heavenly conflicts laid bare.

"Very well," Julian agreed, bowing his head. "I will move my men outside."

CHAPTER 30

∽

And so, when Tallyrand emerged from Eugenie's chamber it was to be confronted by the sight of the Abbot, Lisabetta and the grey-eyed man, seated at the small mixing-table in an otherwise empty room.

The minister regarded them for a moment, his sharp gaze betraying nothing of his thoughts. "Ah. To what do I owe this pleasure?"

The Englishman rose to offer his own chair. "I think a discussion may be in order—one that would be of benefit to all parties."

Tallyrand spread his hands. "You can see for yourself that Eugenie and I are fond, and that I did not take advantage of her." He nodded in Lisabetta's direction. "Her sister will also attest to this. You must inform Castlereagh that the story is false, and has been put about by my enemies."

"Perhaps I will, perhaps I will not," the Englishman replied. "But—unfortunately—Eugenie will not long be with us to refute such a distasteful rumor. And whether or not the rumor is true, it would stand as an excuse for Castlereagh to demand that you be banned from the negotiations."

The diplomat shrugged, unconcerned. "Very well—let him ban me; they will not miss me."

"You are modest, sir; certainly, Austria will miss you."

There was a moment of tense, surprised silence; Tallyrand of the ever-shifting allegiances was currently conniving with Austria to undermine both the British and the Russians. If this were to be revealed, the French King would be forced to disavow any knowledge of such, and Tallyrand would be left without a country to represent.

Whilst their guest sat down heavily—clearly reviewing his options—Lisabetta thought it an opportune time to pull out the man's rosary—stolen by Hahn—and slide it across the table. "I must return this to you, monsieur. I fear you will have need of it."

The minister did not even attempt to hide his abject surprise, as he slowly took the beads into his hands. "Where—where did you get this?"

"*El Halcon's* men stole it from your bedside. It serves as a warning—the guerrilla leader knows you conspire with the *Afrancesados* to keep the artwork from the Spanish cathedrals. You may have double-dealt with Napoleon, and the Tsar, and the English, but the Spanish guerrillas are another matter altogether. They have long memories, and longer knives."

The minister took refuge in outrage, and bristled, "You *dare* to threaten me?"

Coldly, Lisabetta replied, "I threaten you with nothing; I only seek to provide you with a means of redemption—you are my niece's father, after all."

His eyes narrowing, Tallyrand countered, "If Napoleon rises again, the *Alfrancesados* will regain the upper hand, and I will have naught to worry about."

Slowly, she shook her head. "Napoleon has no control over the guerrillas, as he already has learned to his sorrow. If such comes to pass, the guerrillas will only be more determined to make you pay."

The grey-eyed man added, "And you would not better your fortunes under Napoleon, in any event. If he came back into power, we would return to the distasteful rumor that you defiled one of Josephine's wards, and she bore a child as a result. The Emperor has a grieving heart when it comes to the late Empress, and he will look for any excuse to come after you. He is another one with a long memory, and a long knife."

And therein lies the double-bind, thought Lisabetta, as the minister was seen to consider his predicament. We are fortunate indeed, that this the man has made himself vulnerable to so many vicious people.

In a more conciliatory tone, Tallyrand offered, "Surely, we can come to terms? What might I offer that could be of interest to you?"

It was clear the Englishman was well-prepared to answer this question, as he ticked off his terms. "The

Afrancescados will return the artwork to the Spanish cathedrals. You will be given a ceremonial position as Grand Chamberlain of France, and you will retire to live a comfortable life with a healthy pension. You will no longer meddle in international affairs."

Tallyrand cocked his head, thinking this over. "How can you give me assurances that *El Halcon* will stand down, even if I agree? He listens to no one."

But it was Lisabetta who replied. "I can make these assurances. I know a Spanish Grandee who has El Halcon's ear, and as long as the heritage of Spain is restored to her cathedrals, he will not look for vengeance."

The minister took a long breath, and absently fingered his rosary as he thought things over. Into the silence, Julian spoke for the first time. "This would seem an opportune time to mention the slavery issue."

"Yes," the Englishman agreed. "England seeks the abolition of slavery, and so does the Catholic Church. Considering the power of these two players, it would not be any hardship to put your own weight behind it, and force the issue through the Congress."

"Bah—you are naïve, sir," the minister replied in a sour tone. "You may as well slit my throat now; they will never agree. It is a miracle they've agreed to as much as they have, and only because they all fear this strange new revolutionary fever that is sweeping the world."

"You will raise the subject, nonetheless."

"I will," Tallyrand agreed. "But you must be

realistic; I can only assure you of a motion, and perhaps a statement in the final treaty that denounces slavery, couched in general terms."

There was a small silence. "Very well," the Englishman agreed. "An outright prohibition may be too ambitious, at this point."

"Exactly," Tallyrand replied. "You overestimate my power—and the will of the participants, no matter how much they may posture."

But at this juncture, Lisabetta spoke up. "You must put some teeth into such a statement, monsieur, so that it cannot be ignored. The treaty must include a term that allows the Knights of Malta to reestablish in Europe."

She could sense both the Englishman's and Dom Julian's surprise at this unexpected demand, but she kept her gaze firmly locked on Tallyrand's.

Slowly, the minster shook his head. "Impossible; Malta is a strategic stronghold for France, and is not negotiable."

Impatiently, Lisabetta shook her head. "I do not speak of Malta; the treaty must allow the Order to reestablish in Europe. All prohibitions against them will be rescinded, and they can continue their work wherever they wish."

"I understand that the Papal States are to be restored to the Pope," the grey-eyed man offered. "An additional provision about the Knights could easily be included as an addendum."

The minister thought about this for a moment, and then nodded. "Very well; the Tsar will not be happy, but far be it for me to impede the works of St. John."

"You must not allow them to cede anything to the Tsar in return, though," Lisabetta warned. "He cannot use it as an excuse to conscript Hanover." This may have seemed a non sequitur, but the Prussian region of Hanover happened to include the City of Gottingen. Carefully, she did not look at Julian.

The Englishman readily seconded this. "A good point; Hanover would make a good buffer against the Tsar's ambitions in Prussia, and England already has an interest in Hanover's neutrality."

Tallyrand cautioned, "The Tsar is going to wind up with much of Prussia, regardless."

"Hanover must remain independent," the Englishman repeated. "Castlereagh will back you."

Their guest was seen to sigh. "I have my orders, then," he said. "Are we finished?"

"One more request, monsieur," Lisabetta added. "You will marry Eugenie, so that Angelique is your legitimate issue."

All three men stared at her in surprise for a moment, before Tallyrand ventured, "My dear mademoiselle; I am already wed."

But Lisabetta shook her head slightly. "Your wife divorced her first husband, and therefore her second marriage to you would be considered invalid, in the eyes of the Church."

There was a moment of silence, and then Julian spoke. "A reasonable request, certainly. It would also serve to counter any accusations about the child's conception, if the issue ever arose. No one need know immediately."

"Very well," the minister agreed, slapping his hands on the table. "I have no objection."

"I will summon the Hospitaller," said Julian.

CHAPTER 31

And so, Lisabetta went in to inform Eugenie of this latest turn of events, as the Hospitaller was fetched to perform the ceremony.

"I'm to marry Charles?" her sister asked in all astonishment. "And he has *agreed*? Betta, what on earth have you done?"

Lisabetta took her sister's hand in hers. "I do this mainly to protect Angelique, dearest; I want her to have a life that is different than ours—I don't want her to be thought of as a lesser being."

Gently, her sister chided, "We are not lesser beings, Betta. I am ashamed of you for even thinking such a thing."

But Lisabetta only replied, "You haven't traveled in the circles I have, Genie. I lived amongst the other players—and held my own—but despite that, I had no—no *stature*, I suppose you could say; and I was often ill-treated because of it." She frowned, trying to find the words. "I looked into their world from the outside, and could never even hope to be allowed inside."

"We must make the best of what we are given," Eugenie gently reminded her.

Nodding, Lisabetta agreed, "I know, and I think I did make the best. And if Angelique had not been born, perhaps it would not have mattered as much to me, but it seems of all things unfair—that so many doors will be closed to her, and that men will believe there will be no repercussions if they take advantage."

Eugenie issued a dry little chuckle. "I'd like you to name the man who dared to take advantage of either one of us, Betta."

Lisabetta smiled. "No one dared, but only because Josephine threw her mantle of protection over us— and everyone marveled at it, which only proves my point. And—despite Josephine's protection—we were nevertheless used as pawns with little regard to how it affected our future. We truly had few choices."

Softly, Eugenie conceded, "This has always stung for you—much more than for me."

Fingering her sister's hand, Lisabetta bent her head. "I hated the feeling that I was something less, I suppose—and that an honorable marriage was not even an option."

Her sister smiled slightly. "One person in particular comes to mind—but that was hopeless to begin with, dearest."

With her own answering smile, Lisabetta

revealed, "You underestimate me, Genie. Now I will astonish you and tell you that the Abbot has proposed."

Eugenie's stared at her sister. "Willingly?"

Lisabetta laughed. "Willingly."

"How *on earth* did you manage it?"

"Because I learned planning and patience from the masters of the game. And I took careful note of what motivated everyone, and used it to my own benefit."

Softly, Eugenie chuckled in delight. "I am happy for you, Betta—so very happy."

"We will take Angelique, when the time comes, and she will live a happy life, secure in her own family—and not as some other family's stray-relation."

"Thank you," her sister said softly, tears glistening in her eyes. "I could not hope for more."

Lisabetta rose, and briskly moved on to practical matters. "Come, the hour grows late, and you must prepare for your wedding. Can you stand, do you think?"

"I am not sure, and so I think I will sit up in bed, instead."

As Lisabetta helped her sister sit up, Eugenie ventured, "Should Angelique attend me?"

"I think not, dearest. She wouldn't understand the significance, and besides, I'd like to obscure the date when the ceremony actually took place. We will pretend it was a *fait accompli* from before her birth, but necessarily secret in light of the shame it would bring to the groom's civil wife."

Eugenie chuckled. "A fine tale—you have been thinking about this."

"No easy task, to out-think all these others."

"Nonsense; you have always been able to out-think the rest of us." Reaching for her hand, her sister said sincerely, "*Mille mercis*."

Smiling, Lisabetta bent to kiss the top of her head. "*De rien, ma chère.*"

Upon emerging from the sickroom, Lisabetta saw that Tallyrand was engaged in casual conversation with the grey-eyed man, and that Julian was tucking Angelique into one of the infirmary beds, since the child was asleep on her feet. The Abbot's profile was illuminated by the candlelight as he bent over the sleeping child, and she suddenly felt as though her heart stopped for a moment, upon seeing this glimpse into her future. Blinking away her own tears, she thought, *mille mercis,* even though she wasn't convinced there was a God, in the first place. *Mille, mille mercis.*

Watching Lisabetta's gaze, Talleyrand paused to take snuff. "A very pretty child. I will settle a dowry upon her, and then we shall see."

"You will do no such thing," Lisabetta replied in a tart tone. "It would only sink her chances."

He smiled in amusement. "You wound me, my dear."

Gesturing toward the antechamber, she advised, "Come, monsieur; your bride awaits."

With dark humor, he offered, "I will admit that my wedding was the last thing I expected, this night," and he began to limp toward the room.

But even as they approached the antechamber's entry, the door to the infirmary suddenly banged open, and they all turned in alarm to behold Hahn, supporting the proctor—the man clearly suffering from grievous injuries, his bruised face cut and bleeding.

"Who is this?" the Englishman asked sharply.

"The Abbey's proctor," Julian replied, swiftly crossing over to help Hahn support the stricken man. "Speak, then."

"No one was to enter," Lisabetta rebuked Hahn in exasperation.

"He tells of treachery," Hahn explained, thoroughly alarmed. "You must listen."

CHAPTER 32

Through his one good eye—the other was swollen shut—the proctor surveyed the assembled personages with some surprise, but then his gaze fell upon Lisabetta, and he managed to gasp, "It was the—the fishmonger, Antoine. He—he was watching the Abbey, and he seized me when I attempted to return. I carried a letter from—from my master, and they took it—"

"You must sit down, and let us tend to your wounds," Lisabetta interrupted his recitation, and tried to give him a warning glance.

Swaying slightly, the proctor blinked at her, trying to focus as the Englishman demanded, "Who beat you?"

"One of Antoine's fishermen—he beat me, and demanded that I tell him—"

Here, he suddenly paused, as though finally becoming aware that he was speaking a bit too freely;

his gaze skewing around the room at the assembled listeners.

"Tell him what?" Julian asked impatiently, giving him a little shake. "Speak, man."

"That the Tsar of Russia siphons the treasure of St. Alban's," Lisabetta answered. There was nothing for it, and it would be best if everyone was made aware; if Rochon's people now knew, it did not bode well; they would be infuriated by the idea that the Tsar was enriching himself with French treasure.

"*What?*" Tallyrand expostulated, understandably unhappy. "For shame, Lisabetta; you cannot give away the treasure to others—promises were made to me."

"Promises were made to everyone," Lisabetta admitted.

But the proctor's gaze had focused on Tallyrand, and now the injured man gazed upon the diplomat with increasing incredulity. "You! What do *you* do here?"

Recovering his sangfroid, the minister bowed. "Why, my good man; I am here to marry Eugenie."

Bewildered, the proctor asked, "Who is 'Eugenie'?"

"No one a'tall," the minster replied smoothly.

"There appears to have been a small misunderstanding," the Englishman observed in a brusque tone, and then addressed Hahn. "Perhaps you should retreat to high ground."

He doesn't like this, and wants Hahn to signal for

reinforcements, Lisabetta thought; and small blame to him—I don't like this, either.

But matters were to take yet another dramatic turn, as the proctor stared at the Englishman. "You," he breathed. "Antoine told me who you are."

"He is mistaken," the Englishman replied, almost kindly.

"Careful—" Lisabetta warned the grey-eyed man in English, but it was too late; with a quick gesture, the proctor pulled Hahn's pistol from his belt, and quickly backed away, wild-eyed. "You—you all conspire against my master!"

"Set a signal," the Englishman repeated to Hahn, and the Indiaman immediately turned to dash out the door.

For a moment, the proctor aimed the weapon at the retreating man, but hesitated, knowing he'd only have the one shot before he'd have to reload. Bleeding and sweating, the whites of his eyes showed as he whirled to point the pistol at Tallyrand. "If anyone should die, it is you!"

"I don't believe we've met," Tallyrand offered, spreading his hands in a friendly fashion. "Perhaps we should have a glass of wine, and discuss the matter."

But Julian stepped in front of Tallyrand, so as to shield him. "Frederick," he said to the proctor, his voice sympathetic, but containing a hint of steel. "You forget yourself. Come; let us attend to your injuries."

Lisabetta held her breath; Julian couldn't let the

man murder Tallyrand—not before the minister had performed his assigned tasks at the Congress.

Taking a cautious step toward the desperate man, Julian held out his hand for the pistol whilst Tallyrand and the Englishman wisely stayed silent. The proctor retreated a step as his wild gaze skewed around the room—seeking a way out—and then chanced upon the sleeping child in the bed behind him. Immediately, he leveled the pistol at Angelique as he quickly backed away so as to pull her bodily out of bed, the surprised child blinking in the candlelight.

Whilst Lisabetta watched in horror, the man then held the whimpering child before him like a shield, his pistol to her head. "I—I demand safe passage, immediately."

"Frederick—" began Julian in the same calm tone, and he took another relentless step; Lisabetta was certain that he hoped to draw the man's fire, so that the others could take him down.

Since this plan was unacceptable to Lisabetta, she interrupted him. "My dear friend," she addressed the proctor, her hands spread at her sides. "You are upset, and rightly so. I will guarantee safe passage—there is no one here who dares to say me nay. Only put the poor girl down."

"No! You are here, meeting with them!" the man retorted, nearly hysterical with rage. "You lie!"

"Come," said Julian again, in a reasonable tone. "You forget that Antoine and his men await you outside. I will guarantee you safe passage to the river

—my oath on it. There is no need to frighten the child."

"Stay back," the proctor demanded, his confidence growing as he saw that they were all stymied; with a quick glance at the door, he began to sidle toward it, the pistol's muzzle firmly pressed against the weeping child's blond curls.

Frantically, Lisabetta reviewed her options and decided she would rush him and risk a shot—he was not the steady sort, after all—but before she could act, they heard a sound similar to a fist-blow, and the proctor's eyes suddenly widened in frozen horror.

Julian immediately lunged forward to wrest Angelique from his grasp, as the little man staggered a few steps and then collapsed forward, the short shaft of a feathered arrow protruding from his back.

His collapse revealed the frail figure of Eugenie, standing in the doorway to her chamber, and leaning against the stone jamb as she lowered a crossbow, resting its tip against the floor. Into the silence, she whispered, "Someone will have to help me reload."

CHAPTER 33

"Well done," said the Englishman in a brisk tone, as he stepped forward to take the pistol from the proctor's lifeless hand.

"Oh—oh, Genie," Lisabetta exclaimed, running to support her sister. "It is just like old times."

"Let me take her back to bed," said Julian, who'd taken the woman's other arm.

But their relief was short-lived, as there was a sudden pounding on the infirmary door. "Open," commanded a man's voice.

"Antoine!" Lisabetta called out to him, running toward the door. "You must find the Indiaman—quickly; he steals the treasure. He is on the premises, somewhere—hurry, I dare not open the door."

"You lie!" a furious Antoine shouted back. "I know the truth, now—you conspire with the Tsar."

"No, no—it is the Indiaman—please, you must believe me, Antoine. He will escape; you must take your men and stop him at the river."

"I will hear no more of your lies," the man shouted, and suddenly they could hear other men with him, and the sound of forceful blows, hitting the heavy door.

Lisabetta retreated back to the others in the room. "*Peste*, where is Hahn?" she exclaimed impatiently. "He could draw them off."

"It doesn't sound as though they would be drawn," the Englishman advised in a terse tone. "But we have reinforcement on the river, and he has signaled to them—we have only to wait, and hope the door holds."

And hard on his words, they beheld the welcome figure of the Indiaman, as he nimbly dropped down from one of the high windows that lined the room. It seemed to Lisabetta, however, that Hahn's expression was uncharacteristically grave.

The grey-eyed man must have noticed the same, because he asked in a sharp tone, "What has happened?"

"I signaled, and signaled again, but there was no responding signal," the man reported.

The Englishman swore softly, and Lisabetta glanced at him in dismay. Tremaine—for reasons which could easily be guessed—was not paying attention.

The Englishman ordered in a clipped tone, "Then go—climb out, and get down to the river to raise them yourself."

"There is no time," Julian countered, as the

assault on the infirmary door continued pounding away. "And we cannot put our visitor at risk."

"Amen," Tallyrand offered fervently.

"What do you suggest?" the Englishman asked, since it seemed clear the Abbot had an alternate plan.

To Hahn, Julian asked, "Do you think you can scale down the tower?"

"Of course, I can," Hahn replied, as though he was insulted by the very question.

"Run up, then; there is a bucket of chemicals near the far wall—spill it over the documents that are stacked upon the table, but take care not to spill any on yourself. Go to the window sill, and throw a lantern onto the table; be ready to drop down immediately—there will be an explosion. It will make an unmistakable signal, and even if your men do not see it, the village will be roused."

At Hahn's glance, the Englishman nodded his agreement. "Go."

They watched Hahn run toward the tower stairway, as the pounding on the door continued—the door creaking a bit ominously under the hard blows.

The Englishman then said to the Abbot, "The fire will serve as an excellent diversion; where is the escape route?"

Julian was silent, and—a bit puzzled by the question—Lisabetta suggested, "We can go down the steps and lock ourselves in the strong-room until reinforcements arrive—that should keep us secure."

"No; it is paramount that our visitor escape

without being seen," the Englishman explained, his steady gaze on Julian. "No one can discover what has transpired here—or even be aware that he was present. I imagine the Abbot knows of a secret passageway; this is not the Abbey's first siege."

Bowing his head in acquiescence, Julian affirmed, "There is a hatch on the floor of the strong-room. A tunnel exits out into the forest."

Lisabetta stared in surprise as the Englishman nodded. "To the strongroom, then; there is no time to waste."

Hard on his words, they all started as the infirmary door finally began to splinter. "Load the crossbow," Eugenie urged. "I will wait, and shoot whoever comes first through the door. It will hold them off long enough for the rest of you to escape."

"No," Lisabetta protested immediately.

"Do as I say, Betta," her sister replied in a firm tone. "And allow me to be useful, one last time."

"An excellent idea," said Julian, as he crossed over to pick up the crossbow, and pluck another arrow from the rack on the wall. "Here you are."

But instead of handing her the weapon, he hoisted Eugenie over his shoulder and whirled toward the room's far end. "Follow me," he said to the others.

CHAPTER 34

Grasping Angelique's hand, Lisabetta hurried along with the others as they followed Julian, who carried a protesting Eugenie down the winding stone steps beneath the tower.

"Let me carry the crossbow," the Englishman urged Julian.

"No," replied the Abbot.

Mon Dieu, save me from nettlesome men, thought Lisabetta. "I can carry it, Julian."

"No need; here we are." They'd arrived at the strong-room door, and—balancing his burden—Julian reached within his tunic to pull forth a ring of keys, one of which he fitted into the fortified oaken door. The Englishman stepped forward to assist as they pulled on the door's iron ring, but his assistance wasn't much needed because the heavy door opened easily, on well-oiled hinges.

And it was just in time; they could hear shouts of

triumph overhead as the infirmary door finally broke down and Antoine's men poured into the infirmary.

Quickly, the Englishman helped Julian close the heavy door, and—after the Abbot turned the key in the lock—they all paused for a moment in relieved silence.

"Where is the tunnel?" asked Tallyrand, taking a glance around the stone-walled room.

"We must move these chests," Julian directed; "The hatch is beneath them."

Tallyrand was seen to pause, apparently much moved as he laid a reverent hand on the stacked chests. "The St. Alban's treasure?"

"D'accord," Lisabetta affirmed solemnly.

"May I see?" the minister wheedled. "I would dearly love a souvenir, and I am certain the King would not object; I represent him, after all."

"You represent no one but yourself, monsieur," Lisabetta retorted dryly.

"Then we are kindred spirits, you and I, and I should have a souvenir to commemorate our evening together."

With a smile, Lisabetta nodded her acquiescence. *"Bien*; take something then, with my compliments."

Carefully, the minister lifted the top casket's lid to reveal oilskin bags, laid within. After loosening one sack's drawstring, he drew-in his breath as he gently shook-out a glistening tangle of ruby-set jewelry.

For a moment, they were all silent, and then the minister remarked, "I should have married you in truth, Eugenie."

Eugenie chuckled in her thready voice. "Josephine would have never allowed it, Charles—she knew you too well."

"God keep the Empress," the man replied in a pious tone, and then lifted a ruby necklace with reverent fingers. "It is fortunate for me that she preferred sapphires."

"Mam'selle Betta," Angelique insisted in an urgent whisper. "We forgot my dolls."

And here, thought Lisabetta, is a very good reminder of what is important, and what is not. She bent to reassure the girl, "I will fetch them myself, dearest—my promise. Only now we must have an adventure, and climb though the floor. Can you do it?"

Her eyes wide, the girl nodded. "Will Georges come fetch us?"

"I would be surprised if Georges wasn't coming to fetch us at this very moment," Lisabetta assured her. "Let's go meet him."

Julian had moved several more chests aside, and now inserted a lever to pull up a hidden trapdoor that was cleverly set within the stone floor. He lit the lantern that hung on the wall, and handed it to the Englishman, saying, "If you will go first, I will bring up the rear."

"Very well."

The grey-eyed man sat upon the edge of the opening and then jumped down into the darkness. Lisabetta followed him, and then they both raised their hands to receive Eugenie, as Julian handed her down, followed by Angelique, and then finally Tallyrand, who needed some assistance since he wasn't as steady on his feet.

Taking up Angelique's hand once again, Lisabetta followed the Englishman along the silent passage, her eyes straining as the lantern bobbed along in front of her. The tunnel was of hewn rock—which made sense, as it must have been constructed when the Abbey was built—and although it was narrow, there was enough room to stand upright—no doubt to allow for provisions to be carried in or out as necessary. As they made their way in the darkness, she couldn't help but think about all the others who'd used this ancient passageway over the centuries, and of the careful planners who'd put it there.

Lost in thought, she was taken completely by surprise when she heard the Englishman suddenly grunt, and then she nearly stumbled over his crumpled form because the lantern had fallen to the ground. In acute dismay, she looked up to behold the figure of Jacques, leaping over the fallen man so as to close with her.

CHAPTER 35

"Ware!" she called out frantically, before the big man's arms closed around her, and lifted her bodily off her feet.

She could hear Tallyrand's shout of dismay as she struggled to pull her blade from her sleeve, but her attacker was wise to this tactic now, and pinned her firmly against him, wresting her knife into his own hand.

"Julian, it is Jacques," she warned, afraid to shout too loudly, for fear there were others nearby—Rochon's men rarely worked alone.

"Quiet," Jacques growled, as he held the knife to her throat. She could sense his sudden uneasiness, as he paused to gaze upon Tallyrand in the flickering lantern light, with Eugenie and Angelique lined up behind him. In a menacing tone, he warned, "You will tell me what you do here."

"Put her down," said Julian, pushing forward through the others. With a deliberate motion, he lifted the crossbow, and aimed it at Jacques—even though the man held Lisabetta against his chest. "This does not concern you."

As the Englishman regained his wits, he struggled to his hands and knees and Jacques backed further away from them, blocking the passageway and holding Lisabetta so tightly that she could scarce catch her breath.

"The Abbey is afire," Jacques said.

"Yes," Julian replied. "We must all get clear; let her go."

But the big man only gave Lisabetta a little shake, for emphasis. "Let her go so you can kill me? I think not."

"I will not kill you," Julian promised.

"Shoot—shoot them both," the Englishman rasped out. "He is going to kill her anyway."

"No!" Eugenie protested, horrified.

Julian was seen to hesitate, and Lisabetta met his eyes in a silent message, ready to collapse her weight so as to give him a decent shot at the man who held her.

"Do it, man," the Englishmen insisted.

"No," Julian replied, as he slowly lowered the crossbow. "Jacques is one of mine."

Lisabetta stared at him, for once bereft of words.

"That," said the Englishman, as he managed to regain his feet. "Is quite the surprise."

Jacques, however, seemed reluctant to release Lisabetta, and he addressed Julian, "You may not be aware—"

But Julian interrupted him. "Enough; she can be trusted completely."

With palpable reluctance, Jacques released Lisabetta rather abruptly, so that she staggered a bit. He doesn't like me much, she realized; he probably thinks I'm a bad influence over our Abbot, here. Nonetheless, she murmured, "*Mille mercis*," to her erstwhile attacker, now realizing how Julian must have become aware of Rochon's barrel-plot, all those years ago. "I owe you my life."

Jacques ignored her, and Julian asked him, "What is the situation?"

"Georges is mustering the village to fight the fire."

"The beggars?"

With a sidelong glance at the Englishmen, the man reported, "They have scattered." In a seeming non sequitur, he added, "Their assistance is not needed, since the Indiaman has brought a group of Englishmen to aid the villagers."

But the Abbot only suggested, "Perhaps a few beggars could object to the presence of the English; a melee would provide a needed distraction." He tilted his head in Tallyrand's direction. "It is paramount that we smuggle him out, unseen."

Jacques nodded. "A melee will be arranged. And if you wish, I can take this man to my boat, and hide him under the nets when I travel upriver to make a report. No one would think to search me."

Julian nodded. "Very good."

Taking Tallyrand's arm in his grip, Jacques

instructed, "Come along, monsieur. You will smell of fish by the time this night is over."

In all gratitude, Tallyrand replied, "I will gladly roll in fish oil, sir, if you can extract me from this place."

As Lisabetta and the others watched Jacques and Tallyrand disappear down the tunnel, Julian advised, "We should return back in the direction we came. We don't want to risk drawing attention to them, and the Hospitaller will let us know when it is safe to emerge again."

"Very well," said the Englishman. "And you have my promise that I will say nothing of Jacques to anyone else."

"Be assured; I will know if you do," the Abbot replied in an even tone.

As Lisabetta took up Angelique's hand yet again, she was thankful for the darkness, so that no one would see that she rolled her eyes.

CHAPTER 36

"How does your head?" Lisabetta asked the Englishman. She was leaning against the rock wall in the darkened tunnel, Eugenie's head cradled on her lap since her sister had fallen into an exhausted slumber. Julian sat beneath the hatch with Angelique asleep on his own lap, as they waited for the all-clear.

The grey-eyed man had sat at a small distance for a while, but now he sidled closer to her, and she guessed that she knew why; as she'd told Hahn, the spymasters may be ruthless by necessity, but that didn't meant they didn't indulge in a small measure of regret, on occasion. And only if there was no disadvantage to it, of course.

Answering her question, the Englishman probed the lump on his head and winced. "I've had worse. Mainly I am disgusted that I was taken by surprise."

"*Tout à fait*; it does not happen often."

In a conciliatory tone, he offered, "I hope you are not unhappy that I sought to skewer you."

"No," she acknowledged with a small smile. "You'd little choice; I would have done the same."

"Good." He glanced at her. "You didn't know of Jacques?"

"No."

"The Abbot plays his cards very close to the vest, it seems. I wonder what else we don't know?"

She eyed him, amused. "Nothing that I would tell you, monsieur."

"No—I suppose you are loyal to him; it only stands to reason. Although you did not tell him of the proctor, I think—you certainly didn't tell me."

"*C'est vrai*," she agreed, and offered nothing further.

He chuckled. "You are a rare woman, Lisabetta, in that you keep your own counsel."

She shrugged slightly. "It has served me well."

"As we have seen," he agreed. "I am more optimistic about a lasting peace than I have been in quite some time."

She glanced over at him. "Will Tallyrand hold faith, do you think?"

"I think he will. He has little choice; he's caught in a double-bind, and we gave him a satisfactory exit. Castlereagh will be doing cartwheels, to be rid of him." He lowered his gaze, and examined the stone floor for a moment. "Were the rubies genuine?"

"As if I would tell you," she chided.

"I only ask out of self-interest." His gaze slid to hers.

"You will be paid," she assured him. "And with genuine stones."

"England will be paid," he corrected gently.

"*D'accord*. And I will say in turn, that you are a rare breed of man, monsieur, to be so loyal to your country." She knew—better than anyone, perhaps—of the offers that had been thrown his way, in a futile attempt to divert him from his objectives. In a way, it was similar to the offers that had been thrown her way, and which had been just as futile—although in her case she loved a man, and not a country.

Naturally, he ignored her comment and instead said, "It will be much-appreciated, this treasure of yours. Your contribution will help shore-up the peace."

She sighed. "I think peace is a mirage, monsieur —it is always just beyond the horizon, and just beyond our grasp. I ask only that you keep the Hanover region peaceful for the next few years—this I would greatly appreciate."

He cocked his head, curious. "You have shown a surprising interest in keeping Hanover out of the Tsar's hands."

"I have my reasons."

Glancing at her, he persisted, "It pains me to think you know something I don't."

"It is a personal matter, monsieur. Nothing of import to you."

"You can't trust me," he acknowledged.

Leaning her head back against the wall, she let out a breath. "Ah—but I do trust you; it is why I enlisted you in this gambit to begin with. You are honorable, like Julian, and—although you both seem a bit foolish to me, at times—I can admire your predictability, even at no small cost to yourselves. In fact, I will tell you something that is worth more than my treasure, perhaps. Despite all appearances, the Baron Corvairre conspires with the Tsar against the King of France."

But the Englishman remained unperturbed, and replied, "You assume I do not already know this."

Slowly, she shook her head. "I do not think that you do, else you would not have the good Baron on your own payroll."

There was a small pause, and he bowed his head in concession. "Many thanks."

"*De rien.*"

They sat for a moment in companionable silence, and then she asked, "What will happen to Tremaine?"

"He will be discharged. We can ill-afford a weak link."

She made a sound of sympathy, even as she knew the spymaster had little choice. "He has family in Wales, I think; they held a mining company he was hoping to avoid."

"Not my concern."

"No," Lisabetta agreed, and thought again of what she'd warned Hahn.

"On the other hand, I will miss you sorely,

Lisabetta. If it doesn't work out with the Abbot, I will be waiting in the wings; you have only to ask for me at The Moor's Head Tavern."

"Now, *there* was a good melee," she reminisced.

He chuckled, "No need to sound so wistful; if we married, you could continue to destroy barware whenever you pleased."

But with a smile, she only shook her head. "No—I will be cooking dinner and tending babies. But I thank you for the offer, just the same."

His chest rose and fell. "Then I will take this opportunity to say *adieu*, Lisabetta. It has been a pleasure."

"Yes. *Adieu*, monsieur."

And with that, they settled into silence.

CHAPTER 37

And so, two days later Lisabetta found herself at Georges' house and a married woman. Julian had insisted the Hospitaller marry them immediately, and she could only be grateful that her *tête-à-tête* with the grey-eyed man had apparently sparked another flare of jealousy.

The damage from the fire was mainly to the Abbey's tower, and even that was repairable, since the building was made of stone that had withstood far worse, and on multiple occasions. In the meantime, they'd moved Eugenie and Angelique to Georges house, and waited to hear word that Julian was discharged from his duties and could transfer to the wilds of Prussia, to serve his Order in an entirely different way.

At present, they were lying in bed, recovering from another round of lovemaking—the hour was rather advanced, but the Abbot was showing no inclination to rise. As she nestled into his chest,

Lisabetta smiled to herself; after their midnight wedding they'd been too exhausted to do anything but fall into bed and sleep, but early the next morning she'd awakened to a warm hand exploring her curves, and in the ensuing two days her new husband had shown a rather impressive interest in keeping a mattress to her back.

They were still becoming familiar with each other, and she'd been careful not to do anything that would shock the poor man—indeed, it was entirely possible she'd never do such things again. She'd no regrets, and instead relished the sense of pent-up satisfaction that Julian had exhibited as he'd become acquainted with the basics—his poor Confessor must have tired of hearing about lustful thoughts, over the years.

Unless he'd not had lustful thoughts, of course— it was possible; he was a man very much in control of himself, as they'd all seen on that night-of-nights.

Thinking on this, she broke the silence. "I am sorry all your work was destroyed, Julian. It must have pained you to send Hahn to light the fire."

His chest rose and fell beneath her cheek. "I will reconstruct most of the data—and I am not the only one who has documented similar experiments."

She smiled. "You will be happy to be living amongst your own, I think."

But he only corrected in a mild tone, "I lived amongst my own at the Abbey, also."

"Yes. You are like me, and can fit into many different roles."

Idly, his fingers caressed her back. "I suppose that

is true. And now you will be a hausfrau, in Hanover."

She turned her head to kiss his chest. "It will be my greatest role. As long as your Order allows it, of course." This was something of a concern for her, as she didn't half-trust his superiors in St. Petersburg.

But he seemed confident. "They will; they are grateful for the funding you have provided over the years. And I made certain to let them know that the proctor threatened my life, and to inquire how such an unstable man came to be appointed in my household."

"You should be in Vienna," she observed in all admiration. "You know how to make a threat, and couch it behind polite words."

He squeezed her in gentle admonishment. "Why didn't you tell me that the proctor was the Tsar's man?"

She'd been expecting the question, and was rather surprised he'd waited this long to ask it. "Much better to play along, and help fashion the information that was being reported back to his master." She lifted her head, to meet his gaze. "And what could you have done, even if you'd known? Your hands were tied, but mine were not. I made certain his master left you alone."

"I would have liked to have known, regardless," he insisted. "You would feel the same, in my place."

"That is a very good point," she agreed thoughtfully, as she fingered his chest. "And in turn, I would have like to have known that Jacques was your man. I suppose we will have to trust each other, going forward—although if I were truly concerned about the proctor, I would have told you, Julian; we were lucky he was not very bright. *Tiens*, neither the Tsar nor the Englishman sent us their best, and it is all rather insulting."

"I imagine everyone's 'best' are occupied elsewhere, if the rumors about Napoleon are true."

She frowned slightly. "The Englishman believes the Emperor will not prevail; he hasn't enough money."

"The Englishman would probably know."

This seemed a perfect opening, and so she ventured, "The only piece of jewelry that remains is the Apostle's necklace, but I think that is the one thing that should not be bartered back and forth, like a child's game. I was thinking of donating it to the British Museum, in the Englishman's family name."

She waited with some trepidation for his reaction, but he only said, "It is yours to do with as you wish. Lisabetta."

She lifted her head to gaze at him again. "You will not be resentful?"

He smiled, and leaned forward to kiss her forehead. "How can I? It is a small consolation for him; I have carried off the prize."

To reward this sentiment, she moved atop him to kiss him in a lingering fashion. "You are a generous man." She nuzzled his throat, and murmured, "As I have seen twice already, this morning."

He chuckled, but it seemed he was not yet ready

for a third round, as he asked, "What is the Englishman's family name? No one seems to know."

"I keep my secrets, husband," she teased, and laid her cheek against his chest, relishing the feel of him beneath her. She'd dreamed of lying thus for a long, long, time, and at last, here she was. It was truly her greatest gambit, by far—not to mention that she'd worked like a horse in harness to bring it about.

His chest rose and fell. "I must be grateful to the Englishman, it seems. And the English have been at the forefront of the slavery fight—another point in their favor."

"Your Order should turn Protestant, perhaps; the Knights and the English would make a formidable pairing."

He chuckled, and she chuckled also, even though she'd been half-serious. Leave it to the men, to be rigidly constrained; unlike women, who've had to remain flexible as a necessity for thousands of years.

Idly, he stroked her back, his fingers light. "*El Halcon* didn't know anything about this, did he?"

Impressed that he'd guessed, she shook her head. "No. But the guerrillas are intent upon returning the Spanish artwork to the cathedrals, one way or another—that much was true."

"So; you did *El Halcon* a favor, in that the artwork will be returned without his firing a shot."

"*Enfin*, it was he who did us a favor. He makes a very good *bête noire*."

"Who stole the rosary?"

"I must not say," she chided in gentle

remonstrance. "And so, you must not ask."

"Your pardon." But her comment seemed to invoke a more serious line of thought, and he chose his words with care. "It may be strange for you, Lisabetta, to be out of the game, and not gathering-up the secrets of powerful men. You may eventually regret having stepped away, and chafe at living a more mundane life."

She lifted her head to meet his eyes—the expression within them a bit somber—and readily smiled her reassurance. "I will have no regrets at all; I am sick to the teeth of intrigue—even though it has paid me well. Which reminds me; my pearls are worth a goodly sum, and you will need to build a new laboratory in Gottingen."

With a gentle hand, he pulled her head to rest it on his chest again. "You must keep your pearls; they will make a fine tale to tell our children."

Supremely content, she lay upon him in silence for a few moments, and then they both chuckled to hear Angelique outside the window, calling out for her Aunt Betta before Georges hurriedly hushed her, and moved her away. The little girl had spent the past two days playing outside in the yard, with a fond Eugenie watching her; because the treasure—or what remained of it—had been secured by the Knights, she was no longer at risk.

Lisabetta said, "I'd like to take Eugenie to the riverbank, today. We will sit and watch the boats sail past."

"Shall I join you, or would you rather it be just the

two of you?"

"You must come, also—and Angelique, too. We are all a family, now—it is a wonderful thing, and perhaps something you cannot quite understand; we were never a family, before—instead, we were an embarrassing footnote to someone else's family. And Josephine may have been a generous protector, but it did not change the fact that we were something less." She paused, and then added softly, "It is the one gift I wanted to give to Eugenie, before she is gone."

He leaned to kiss her. "Eugenie has given me the same gift."

Much struck, Lisabetta could only agree. "*Tiens*, I suppose you are right. Had she not had Angelique—or fallen ill—I would never have thought-up my gambit."

"*Deo Gratias*," he said quietly.

"Yes," she agreed. "Eugenie may die far too soon, but now her daughter will have an ordinary life; she can marry a good man, and never feel that she is less-than."

"I am not certain that you would have been content with an ordinary life, Lisabetta."

"I was never given the opportunity to test it, though. And so, I wished something better for Angelique."

He reached to kiss her, again. "We can only hope that she has her aunt's courage."

"I must disagree, *mon Abbé*," she replied with a smile. "My hope is that she never has to be brave at all."